Space watchman Vorgens comes to Shinar to bring peace, yet he finds himself caught up in a violent conflict of interests. Cast in the rôle of mutineer, military commander and lover, Vorgens grows up fast. But will even he be able to control the devastation and bloodshed which the outburst of alien hostilities brings? Only Vorgens can save the Empire: will he do it . . .?

Star Watchman

BEN BOVA

SPHERE BOOKS LIMITED
30/32 Gray's Inn Road, London WC1X 8JL

First published in Great Britain by Dobson Books Ltd 1972
Copyright © Ben Bova 1964
Published by Sphere Books Ltd 1977

Set in Monotype Baskerville

Printed in Great Britain by
Hazell Watson & Viney Ltd
Aylesbury, Bucks

To the one and only Rosa

CONTENTS

CHAPTER ONE

SHINAR

The Terran Empire stretched over half the Milky Way galaxy, from the lonely fringes of the immense spiral of stars to its richly-packed center. Earth was the capital of this vast Empire, but the planet Mars was headquarters for the Star Watch. The Empire's military arm, the Star Watch had bases on many planets, in all the farthest reaches of the immense Terran domain. But Mars – covered from pole to pole with mighty buildings housing the men and machinery that ran the Star Watch – was headquarters.

In a small office in one of those buildings, a noncom was startled out of his usual routine. His desk communicator lit up, and the dour features of the Chief-of-Staff took form on the screen.

'I want the complete file on Oran VI immediately.'

'Yes sir.' Before the chief's image had completely faded from the screen, the noncom's fingers were tapping out a message on his desktop keyboard to the mammoth computer that held the Star Watch's master files.

He decided to check and make certain that he had requested the correct information from the computer. (The possibility of the computer making an error was unthinkable.) He punched a button on the desk, and the communicator screen lit up again.

The screen showed a map of the Milky Way galaxy, with the position of the star Oran marked out. It was on the edge of the Terran Empire, out in one of the farther spiral arms of the galaxy, near the territory of the Komani nation. The map faded, and a block of written data filled the screen:

ORAN: galactic coordinates ZJJ27458330194126-3232. Eight planets, one terrestrial (Oran VI).

ORAN VI: radius 1.04, density 0.91, gravity 1.025. Atmosphere Earth-normal (0.004 deviation). Three major continents, surface 80% sea-covered. Native human population, 3.4 billion (estimated). Economy: rural agricultural; underdeveloped industrial base. Subject to Imperial Development Plan 400R, priority 3C. Former colony of Masters, incorporated into Empire immediately following Galactic War of last century. Native name for planet: Shinar.

'SHI-NAR!'

The square was thronged with people. Shouting, jumping, dancing people. It was hard to see how so many people could jam into the city square, but still more were pouring in from every avenue. They waved banners and held aloft placards. Several groundcars were overturned and swarmed over. A bonfire glowed near a statue at one end of the square. The people shouted one word, which rose and fell like the endless waves of the sea:

'SHI-NAR! SHEE-*NAR*!'

The Terran governor stood frowning on the balcony of his official residence, at the head of the jam-packed square. He turned to the garrison commander standing beside him. 'This has got to be stopped!' The governor had to shout to be heard over the roars of the crowd. 'There'll be another riot down there in a few minutes. The native police can't handle that mob.'

The commander arched his eyebrows. 'Sir, if I send my troops into the square, there may be bloodshed.'

'That can't be helped now,' the governor said. 'Send in the troops.'

Star Watch Junior Officer Emile Vorgens sat in his tiny compartment aboard the starship and reread his orders for the tenth time. He found it hard to believe that he was finally a full-fledged officer of the Star Watch. School was finished, his commission was safely tucked away in his travel kit, and here – on plastic film – were the orders for his first official mission.

He slid the tiny film into his pocket viewer again and projected the words onto the bare compartment wall:

'You will proceed to Oran VI and assist the Imperial Governor there in dealing with certain dissident elements of the native population.'

Like most Star Watch Orders, there was a good deal of meaning in the words that were *not* there. The Star Watch was the Terran Empire's interstellar military arm. In fact, the Star Watch pre-dated the Empire, and existed even back in the old days of the Confederation, more than a century ago.

It had been the Star Watch that fought the successful war against the Masters, the war that had made the Terran Confederation – almost against its own will – the new masters of most of the galaxy. The problems of ruling such a vast territory had been solved only by the creation of the Empire. Now the Star Watch served to control the interstellar space routes. A subsidiary branch, the Imperial Marines, handled any planetborne fighting that had to be done.

Vorgens sat back in his webbed chair and studied his orders, a worried frown on his face. It was a youthful face, with a high forehead. His skin was a golden brown, his closely cropped hair copperish red, his eyes tawny. Although born into the Terran Empire, and fully human, Vorgens was not an Earth-man, but a native of the Pleiades star cluster.

His orders troubled him. To send a Star Watchman to Oran VI meant that the Empire was considering military action there. 'Dissident elements of the native population.' That could mean almost anything. It sounded serious.

Just how serious, Vorgens learned a few days later. A coded message from Star Watch headquarters was beamed to the ship for him. When he decoded it, the order stated:

'The Imperial Governor of Oran VI has been murdered. You will assist Brigadier Aikens, 305th Imperial Marines, in restoring order to the planet.'

The starship hurtled on toward its destination as Vorgens spent his days fretfully trying to get more information on the situation on Oran VI. Very little could be learned. The Imperial Marines had landed there and the planet was in turmoil. Evidently a band of Komani raiders, sensing a chance for battle and looting, had also landed on Oran VI. A few days before reaching the planet, Vorgens received a final change in orders:

'You will seek out the Komani leader and warn him of the consequences of fighting against the Empire. The Komani raiders are to be offered safe conduct back to their homeworld in return for immediately quitting Oran VI. The

Komani leader is to be reminded that all Komani clans have sworn allegiance to the Empire, and he can expect no assistance from the rest of the Komani nation.'

Almost before Vorgens had a chance to digest the news that these orders implied, the starship broke out of subspace and entered an orbit around Oran VI. A planetary shuttle brought him down to the major spaceport, heavily guarded by Marines.

The major in charge outlined the situation to him quickly:

'Things are pretty confused here, Watchman. We control the four major cities on the planet, and this spaceport. The Komani raiders have been shooting up the countryside. There are bands of native rebels with them. Brigadier Aikens has the Mobile Force out hunting down the raiders.'

Without more ado, the major bundled Vorgens into an aircar and sent the Watchman off, with a Marine pilot and gunner, to find Brigadier Aikens and the Mobile Force.

CHAPTER TWO

THE VALLEY

Sergeant McIntyre had come a long way in the heat of the afternoon, scrabbling over the broken rocks, half tumbling down the steep slope of the valley, while the big yellow sun of Oran blazed hotter and brighter every minute.

Finally he saw the first outpost of the Mobile Force – a scout car, its turret hatches open, and a few men sitting lazily in the scant slice of shade the car offered.

As he approached, one of the troopers got up slowly, adjusted his glare visor, picked up his weapon and hailed him:

'Who goes?'

'Sergeant McIntyre, K Company, returning from patrol.'

McIntyre stopped a few paces before the younger man. He could feel the sweat trickling down his flanks.

'Returning from patrol?' the trooper echoed. 'Where's the patrol, Sarge?'

'You're lookin' at it, kid,' McIntyre answered. 'Are we gonna stand here all day? I'm hot, tired, thirsty and I've gotta make a report to my company commander.'

The soldier swallowed his amazement, 'Yeah, sure, Sarge. Come on over to the car.' He turned and bawled out, 'Lieutenant!'

McIntyre trudged over to the shade and squatted down on the bare, dusty ground, leaning his back against the dark, cool metal of the scout car. He took off his helmet, squinted painfully into the shimmering afternoon haze as he mopped his head with a tattered sleeve, then replaced the helmet and slid the glare visor over his eyes again.

One of the men offered him a canteen.

A lean, spotless lieutenant climbed down from the turret and confronted McIntyre.

'Sergeant, are you the man who led this morning's patrol through here and out to the southern edge of the valley?'

'Yes sir,' McIntyre said, getting slowly to his feet.

'Where's the rest of your patrol? You had twenty men, didn't you?'

'Yes sir. The others were all killed or captured, sir.'

'What? Impossible!'

McIntyre shook his head. 'I wish it was impossible, sir. I only wish it was.'

Sergeant McIntyre made his report by tri-di beam from the scout car to the communications center of the Mobile Force's main body, camped down in the heart of the valley.

'Sorry we don't have a vehicle for you,' the lieutenant said a little stiffly, to hide his embarrassment. 'We've been ordered to remain here at the perimeter.'

'That's okay, sir,' McIntyre answered. Then he added, with just a hint of malice, 'I don't mind walkin' back. I'll be going *away* from the Komani for a change.'

By the time he reached the main encampment of the Mobile Force, the hot, yellow sun had sunk behind the hills. The sky overhead was still bright, but the valley itself was now in shadow.

As McIntyre made his way through the maze of land cruisers, dreadnaughts, troop carriers, supply vans and scout cars, it became obvious to him that his own report had been matched by equally bad reports from the other patrols of that morning. None of the guard details took the time to ask his identity. None of the shavetail officers stopped him for a lecture about his no-longer-regulation uniform. They knew where most of his equipment had been left, why he had buckled to his hip an extra sidearm (taken from a dying corporal), whose blood was on his ragged shirt.

The petty routine of military life was finished. They were all too busy with the urgency of self-preservation to bother. They were digging in, all across the valley. The Mobile Force of the 305th Imperial Marines, the military extension of the Terran Empire that ruled most of the galaxy, was threatened with annihilation.

It was cooler now that the sun had dipped behind the western hills. That was one thing to be grateful for McIntyre thought as he searched out his company commander in the confusion of men and vehicles. The valley was in shadow, but the hills, where the enemy was, were still bright with daylight.

Surrounded, McIntyre thought to himself. *Totally cut off. I wonder how the Brigadier is taking the news?*

'Totally impossible!' snapped Brigadier Aikens.

'I'm afraid not, sir,' his executive officer answered quietly. 'All the patrols report the same thing – we are surrounded.'

Aikens' pinched face, topped by a balding dome, glowered red as he stared at the stereomap on his desktop viewscreen. 'Are any of the patrols still out?'

'Only two, sir. It doesn't look as though they're going to make it back. The other patrols were badly mauled. One of them lost every man except a single sergeant.'

Aikens got up from his chair and crossed the tiny compartment in three restless strides. Though the dreadnaught was huge for a land-going vehicle, all the compartments inside had to be as compact as humanly possible.

'Surrounded,' he muttered, 'trapped in this valley by a horde of barbarians.'

'They don't fight like barbarians, sir,' the exec murmured.

'What's that?'

The officer flushed. 'I only meant, sir, that they have been using modern weapons – very effectively, sir.'

Aikens nodded. 'I know, I know.' He returned to his desk and sat down again. 'I've led my men into a trap. Now I've got to lead them out of it.' The brigadier stared at the stereomap for a long moment while his aide stood motionless, listening to the faint whirr of the air-conditioning system.

The exec was in his prime middle years, tall and dark-haired. A long stretch of desk duty, as part of the original garrison of Oran VI, had filled out his midsection and softened his face somewhat.

Aikens, although older by at least a dozen years, was straight-backed and flat-stomached. The brigadier had picked his aide on the strength of the younger man's first-hand knowledge of the planet.

Finally Aikens looked up. 'Well, we'll hold our ground tonight. Double the guard around our perimeter.'

'Yes sir.'

'They can maul foot patrols, can they?' the brigadier muttered. 'Tomorrow morning we'll see what they can do against some solid armor.' He looked at the map on his desk again. 'All right, you may go. Make certain you get a verbal report from all the company commanders after the guard is changed, and tell my staff I will meet them here in two hours.'

'Yes sir.'

The exec remained at attention before the desk.

'I said you may go,' Aikens repeated.

'There's one more item, sir. That Star Watch officer who joined the Force two days ago. He's still waiting to see you, sir.'

Aikens slammed a heavy hand on the desktop. 'The situation isn't bad enough! Now I have to put up with shave-tails from the Star Watch Academy who want to peep over my shoulder!'

'Sir, he's been waiting two days, and his orders are direct from Star Watch Headquarters.'

Aikens fumed silently for a few moments, then said, 'All right, get him in here. On the double.'

'Very well, sir.' The exec saluted, turned, and ducked through the low doorway of Aikens' cubbyhole office.

After a few minutes of searching through the dreadnaught's command section, the exec found Vorgens hunched beside a seated technician in the communications compartment, staring intently at a static-streaked viewscreen.

'It's no good, sir,' the technician was saying. 'The enemy has every frequency jammed. We can't get a word in or out.'

Vorgens straightened up. His black-and-silver uniform was in stark contrast to the bright-colored coveralls that identified the crewmen's various jobs aboard the dreadnaught.

'I see,' the Watchman said. 'Thank you anyway.'

'So here's where you've been hiding,' the exec called out. 'Come on, the brigadier wants to see you right away.'

Vorgens stepped out of the communications compartment and into the narrow passageway.

'I've been trying to establish contact with the cities or Star Watch Headquarters. No luck,' Vorgens said as they started down the passageway.

'They've got us boxed in pretty well,' the exec said.

'The reports from the patrols seem to indicate that.'

Vorgens admitted. 'Any chance of signaling to the orbiting ships?'

'What orbiting ships?'

'The transports that brought the Mobile Force here, and their escorts. Perhaps the ships could . . .'

'The ships aren't there, Watchman. They dropped the Mobile Force three weeks ago and left Oran VI immediately. They won't be back until they're called for.'

Vorgens blinked in disbelief. 'But . . . why?'

'It's a big Empire, son,' the exec answered patiently, 'and transports are too valuable to be tied up sitting at one planet, empty and useless.'

'You mean we couldn't retreat off the planet, even if we wanted to?'

'We could commandeer whatever ships are available on the planet, which wouldn't be enough to carry all the men, let alone the equipment. We could get Star Watch ships in a week or so if we could make contact with somebody outside this blasted valley.'

'How in the world did all this come about?' Vorgens wondered out loud.

The exec took him literally and replied, 'It started with some protest demonstrations – some farmers complaining about a nutrient-processing center we were building for them. The next thing we knew, there were riots in the cities. Then the Governor was murdered by some fanatic. The Mobile Force landed a week later, and two days after *that* these Komani hordes landed in half a dozen places across the planet and started terrorizing the countryside. So here we are.'

The exec stopped walking abruptly, and Vorgens realized he was standing before Brigadier Aikens' door.

'You know what I think,' the executive officer stated, rather than asked. 'I think the whole mess is a plan by the Komani to take over this planet, and it's just the first step in a much bigger Komani plan.'

'But they were our allies against the Masters,' Vorgens said.

'That was a hundred years ago, Watchman. Times have changed since then.'

Vorgens nodded.

'Well,' said the exec, 'good luck with the Old Man.'

'You're not coming in with me?'

'No, I've got several chores to carry off before I get my supper. *If* I get a chance to eat tonight.' He flicked a salute at Vorgens and turned away.

Vorgens automatically returned the salute, then turned and confronted the brigadier's door. After an instant's hesitation, he knocked twice.

'Enter.'

He stepped into the compartment, saluted, and stood at ramrod attention. Aikens, sitting behind his desk, regarded the young Watchman for a moment, then indicated with a nod the only other chair in the office. Vorgens sat down.

No two men on Oran VI looked less like each other. Vorgens was small and wiry, and his golden-brown skin and coppery hair proclaimed him to be of non-Earthly stock. His thin, fine-boned face, surmounted by a high forehead, gave him a peculiarly babyish look.

Aikens was a typical Terran, towering above Vorgens' height and outweighing him by half again. The brigadier's only sign of encroaching years was his thinning hair and well-creased face. He had made it a point to foster carefully the impression among his men that he was a flamboyant and daring leader. Even now he was wearing the Imperial Marines' semi-dress uniform of green, red and gold, as opposed to Vorgens' standard Star Watch black-and-silver.

'I imagine you realize the situation we're in,' Aikens said flatly.

Vorgens nodded. 'I have seen the reports of today's patrols.'

'This Mobile Force was dispatched to Oran VI to bolster the Imperial garrison and restore order among the native populace. When the Komani raiders landed, we were ordered to induce them to return to their homeworld. "A demonstration of force": that's how the orders read. Well, for nearly three weeks now we've been trying to pin them down for our little demonstration. Now they've led us into a nasty trap. We're surrounded in this valley, and it looks as though the Komani are perfectly willing and eager to fight a full-scale battle.'

'I know,' Vorgens said.

'They're well armed with modern weapons, and their tactics so far have been masterful. In short, Vorgens, they've led me around by the nose for three weeks, and they're ready to start slugging.'

'Have you any idea of their numbers?'

Aikens shrugged. 'We're outnumbered, that much is certain. How badly, I can't tell. But that doesn't worry me. Trained troops can always lick an undisciplined horde of barbarians, no matter how clever the barbarians are. They may have modern weapons, but we have more firepower . . . and armored vehicles.'

'They seem to have greater mobility, though,' Vorgens observed.

'True enough, and their reconnaissance is much better than ours. What we need is some airpower and a column of reinforcements.'

'Reinforcements?'

'Certainly. Oh, I'm positive we could handle this Komani mob with the men we have right here, but once they start taking a beating, the barbarians will melt back into the hills again and we'll lose them.' Aikens tapped a forefinger on the stereomap as he spoke. 'I want a column of reinforcements, from the city garrisons, with air cover and support, so we can pin down these barbarians from the outside. Then, between our two forces, we can crush them once and for all!'

Vorgens sat in puzzled thought for a moment. Then he said, 'Sir, there are two problems on Shinar: the native rebels, and the Komani raiders. If you strip the cities of their garrisons to hit the Komani, you will be giving the cities to the rebels.'

Aikens shrugged. 'One problem at a time, Watchman. First we crush the Komani. The rebels will be easy to handle after that. Why, we can even show the natives that we helped them get rid of the barbarian invaders. Might win back most of the populace that way.'

'But your aide thinks that the rebels are working for the Komani.'

'True enough. He's probably right. But the majority of the natives don't know that.'

'It's a very mixed-up situation,' Vorgens said.

Aikens smiled grimly. 'We're going to unmix it and make it perfectly simple. The first step is to get the city garrisons marching toward this valley. I'm certain the Komani won't be able to launch a full-scale attack on us for several days. They've got us pinned down, and they'll want us to run out of food and water before they attack. Attrition tactics.'

'Perhaps so,' Vorgens said. 'Now, brigadier, my orders . . .'

'Yes, your orders, that's why I called you in here.' Aikens leaned back in his chair. 'I have a copy of your orders here on my desk, but I'd like to hear how you interpret them.'

'There's not much to interpret.'

'Come now, Watchman,' Aikens countered. 'You've been with Mobile Force for how long now? Two full days, isn't it? Certainly by now you realize that orders cut and processed at Star Watch Headquarters couldn't possibly foresee all the details of the situation here on Oran VI.'

'The orders are quite simple and explicit,' Vorgens insisted. 'I am instructed to attempt to negotiate with the chief of the Komani raiders. I am to tell him that his people can return peacefully to their homeworld if they stop their raiding on Oran VI immediately. I am also to tell him that the Komani clan chieftains have sworn to the Terran Council that they will remain loyal to the Empire and will not in any way aid or sympathize with this attack on Oran VI. I suppose I should remind the raiders that the Komani were allies of the Terrans during the Galactic War of the last century, and that this attack on Imperial territory is a breach of friendship.'

Commander Aikens gazed toward the ceiling as he quietly asked, 'And just how do you propose to contact the Komani chief?'

'That's the difficult part.' Vorgens admitted. 'I had hoped to arrive on this planet before the fighting got so intense that the Komani would refuse to parley. It looks as though I barely made it in time.'

'What do you mean by that?'

'Why, simply that the Komani have not really opened battle yet. We might still be able to discuss a truce.'

'While we're surrounded?' Aiken shook his head. 'You don't understand these barbarians. The only time they're ready to negotiate is when they're taking a beating.'

'My orders command me to attempt . . .'

'Your orders,' Aikens interrupted, 'place you under my command for the duration of your stay on Oran VI. Correct?'

'Yes . . . but with the understanding that as an officer of the Imperial Marines you are subject to the orders of the Star Watch High Command and that you will assist the Star Watch's attempt to bring about a peaceful settlement with the Komani.'

Aikens rose from his chair and strode wordlessly across the small compartment. Then he turned and pointed a finger at Vorgens.

'Listen youngster, I'm just as anxious as you are to talk the Komani out of a bloodletting. Those are *my* men out there, and I'm responsible for their lives – every last one of them. But if we try to parley from our present position – surrounded, cut off, and outnumbered – the Komani will simply take it as a sign of weakness. We'll be encouraging them to attack. We'll be convincing them that they've got us licked.'

'It may be entirely unnecessary to fight at all,' Vorgens insisted.

The brigadier nodded curtly. 'Maybe. We'll see.'

Aikens returned to his desk and sat down. Leaning over the stereomap, he said to Vorgens:

'This is what we're going to do. Tomorrow morning, I'll send out more patrols – stronger patrols than today's — with armor. They'll probe the Komani lines and keep the barbarians off balance. Meanwhile, you will take an armored cruiser and a picked detachment of men and break through the Komani lines.'

Vorgens' mouth dropped open, but the brigadier waved him down before he could say anything. 'You will break through the Komani lines and outrun their communications jammers. Then you will call for reinforcements from the garrisons of the cities we now hold.'

'These are your orders?'

'That's right, Watchman. I'll give you two days and two nights to get the reinforcements here. I doubt if the Komani will attack before then. They've got men scattered halfway across the planet, and they'll want to group them together before they tackle us in earnest.

'You'll have to draw every last man you can get. Use your authority as a Star Watchman. I want a strong enough force to smash these marauding barbarians once and for all.'

'And the truce negotiations?'

'Let *them* make the request for a truce,' Aikens snapped.

'Then you refuse to obey the express orders of the Star Watch High Command?'

Aikens glared at the Watchman. 'What are you trying to do, youngster, set me up for a board of inquiry? No, I do not refuse to carry out the High Command's orders. I simply feel that the situation is so precarious at the moment that the orders can't be put into effect. Not at this time and place.'

Vorgens stood up. 'I suppose it would be pointless to attempt to argue you out of this decision.'

'Completely pointless. Good evening.'

The young Star Watchman saluted and left the brigadier's compartment. He stood outside the door for a moment after closing it, frowning worriedly. Then he slowly made his way down the narrow passage, past the compact booths of officers' quarters, climbed through a hatch and clambered down the side of the dreadnaught to the ground.

It was not much warmer outside than in, now that Oran had set. But the night was never completely dark, despite the hour. Oran was six times brighter than Sol, and its luminosity was great enough to keep a twilight glow in the air all night long.

Vorgens paced slowly around the mammoth dreadnaught, watching his boots stir up the dust. *The Star Watch orders me to parley; the brigadier orders me to fight,* he thought to himself. *Orders are orders. But which set do I obey?*

CHAPTER THREE

FATHER AND SON

Halfway across the planet it was still bright daylight.

The home of Clanthas, the merchant, was neither particularly large nor well-adorned. It stood at the crest of a hill, flanked by equally good houses, and overlooked the harbor of the small city of Katan. Unlike the four major cities of Shinar, the port city of Katan was not occupied by a Terran garrison.

Until a year earlier, Clanthas had been distinguished from his fellow merchants only by being a shade quicker-witted and, perhaps, blessed with slightly more than his share of good fortune. In those days, before the rebellion against the Terran Empire, Clanthas could be seen during most sunny afternoons of the warm summer sitting on the balcony that spanned his house, either relaxing or conducting business, as the occasion demanded.

It was about a year ago that the first farmers began to trickle into Katan, complaining that the Terrans had driven them off their own soil, so that the land could be used for factories that made synthetic foodstuffs.

Clanthas, whose business depended on buying and selling the farmers' produce, appealed to the Terran governor. The nutrient processors were necessary, even vital, he was told.

Instead of quietly trying to make the best of the situation, as most of his countrymen did, Clanthas recalled something his son had told him, some quotation from galactic history that the youth was studying at the university:

'A man is free because he has the brains and the courage to stand on his own feet and go his own way. And for a man to remain free, he and his fellow men must be strong enough to resist those who would enslave them.'

Those words had been spoken more than a century ago by a Terran, Geoffrey Knowland, the conqueror who defeated the Masters and established the Terrans as rulers over Shinar.

Clanthas decided that the Terran's words made sense,

even when applied against the Terrans themselves. So he acted.

He organized the farmers and held a demonstration in Katan. He organized similar demonstrations in the major cities. Inevitably, some of the larger demonstrations developed into riots. Troops were called in; shots were fired. Unarmed civilians were killed. Tempers flared. Violent men took action. The Terran governor was murdered. The Imperial Marines arrived. Komani warriors landed on the planet.

Before he had time to realize it, Clanthas had become the acting leader of his people. He was squarely in an increasingly impossible position. On the one hand stood the Empire-building Terrans, intent on 'pacifying' Shinar and returning it to the status of a docile colony. On the other were the fearsome Komani, with plans of their own. Even among his own people, there were hotheads and opportunists over whom Clanthas had no control.

On this particular afternoon, however, he was trying to put aside thoughts of politics and fighting to confront his only son simply as a bewildered and outraged father.

Clanthas sat on the edge of a large, well-padded chair. He watched intently the image of his son on the screen of the tri-di transceiver in the small room that Clanthas used for private conversations. By the standards of his race, the merchant was in prime middle life. His complexion was nut-brown, his hair dark, his eyes like coal. He had accumulated weight with his years, so that now he was broad-girthed and puffy-faced, but his eyes were still clear and piercing.

His son, Merdon, showed what the merchant must have looked like in his youth: tall, broad, strong-limbed. The two men shared the same facial characteristics – prominent cheekbones, broad brow, massive, stubborn jaw.

'Merdon, I told you this was raving lunacy when you first revealed your idiotic plans to me,' the older man raged. 'I was wrong. It's worse. It's doom. It's damnation. It's the ruin of our planet and our people. And my son – my only son – is the ringleader.'

Merdon shook his head slowly and waited for his father to go on.

'Why couldn't you have trusted my judgment? You, of all

people! You should have remained at my side, and helped me to control your hot-blooded young friends. You should have warned me of the plot against the governor's life. Instead you remained silent. You should have spoken against those who wanted to shoot back at the Terrans. Instead you went even farther.'

'I did what I had to do, Father. The Terrans weren't going to be swayed by mere words.'

'Oh no, you had to be clever. One step ahead of everyone, including your father. Free the planet! Throw the foreigners out! How? By inviting other foreigners in to fight for us. Barbarians!'

'But it's working,' the youth said defensively. 'The Komani have beaten the Terran garrison in several engagements.'

'Yes, and now the Imperial Marines are here.'

'And the Komani have trapped them.'

'WHAT?'

'Didn't you know? The Terrans have been trapped in a valley – in the Carmeer district. The Komani have them surrounded. It's only a matter of time . . .'

Clanthas sank back in his chair. 'Only a matter of time,' he moaned, 'before our planet is completely at the mercy of these barbarians.' He looked up at his son. 'You're certain of this?'

'Okatar Kang is gathering his men from every corner of the planet. Our own fighting units are joining him. There's even talk of contingents from other Komani clans landing on Shinar to join the battle.'

Like vermin attracted to an open wound, thought Clanthas.

Merdon continued, 'Okatar wants to be certain of overpowering strength before we attack the Terrans. We'll wipe them out completely!'

'Listen to me,' Clanthas commanded. 'Keep your men away from that battle. Don't join in it. The Terrans don't realize that we – *you* – invited the Komani to Shinar to fight for us. If they ever find out, they'll never trust any of us again.'

'But . . .'

Clanthas waved his son to silence. 'If the Komani beat the Terrans, they might be weakened enough for us to overcome them. If the Terrans win, we can say we had no active role in fighting against them. Perhaps we can still escape from this circle of doom in which you've placed us.'

'Father, you don't understand. The Komani are our allies. They have come to Shinar because we asked them. They are fighting for *us*. They are dying to help free us from the Terrans.'

The ex-merchant swore under his breath. Aloud, he said, 'The Komani are barbarians. They have no allies. Now they are killing Terrans. Next they will kill Shinarians.'

'Father, you must learn to trust them.'

'I trust them! I trust them to loot this planet when they've finished with the Terrans. I trust them to sack and burn and destroy everything they can't carry away with them, and I trust they'll start just as soon as the Terrans are wiped out.'

'No. They've promised they'll loot only the Terrans.'

'I suppose the villages that they've raided were populated with Terrans.'

Merdon frowned at his father. 'That was a misunderstanding. They needed food, and the stupid farmers refused to feed them. Some of the Komani warriors got out of hand, but we've made arrangements that will eliminate that sort of thing in the future.'

'Fine. And what will your friend Okatar Kang do when he learns that there are warehouses full of food and an arsenal full of equipment right here in Katan?'

'I will protect you,' Merdon said, a slight smile stealing across his face.

Clanthas shook his head. 'No you won't. You'll be dead. If you participate in the coming battle against the Terrans trapped in that valley, you will be killed. Either by the Terrans or the Komani.'

'Father!'

'Don't be naive. You are one of the principal leaders of the rebels. Alive, you are a stubborn, strong-minded, idealistic, capable leader of all the younger idiots of Shinar. You've turned against the Terrans. Someday you will turn against the Komani. But dead – then you'll be a martyr to the anti-Terran cause. The Komani can count on your heroic memory to hold all your rebellious friends in line long past the point where you, yourself, would have broken with them.'

26

'I'm flattered, Father, but you overestimate my importance. The real objective is to free Shinar of the Terrans and their rotten Empire.'

'Free us? And leave the Komani on our backs?'

'They'll leave, after the Terrans have been driven off.'

'And after we're pillaged.'

'No . . .'

'Do you think that the Terrans are going to allow the Komani to escape unpunished? They'll send a stronger force to Shinar. It might even be on its way here at this moment. You're turning your homeworld into a battleground.'

Merdon's face went completely blank. 'There's no point in continuing this argument, Father. You won't change your mind. But someday you'll be proud of your son and the things he will have done for Shinar.'

'I hope so,' Clanthas said wearily, 'but I doubt it.'

The youth said nothing. His body gradually dissolved and disappeared, leaving his father sitting there in silence, staring at the bare screen of the tri-di transceiver.

Merdon also remained sitting before his tri-di set for many minutes after his father's image had faded into nothingness. He frowned moodily, weighing his father's words of warning.

Abruptly, he shook his head and got up from the seat.

'You're a well-meaning old man,' Merdon said softly to his unhearing father, 'but you're hopelessly wedded to the past. The Terrans became our overlords by driving the Masters out of the Galaxy. It took action, force – not words and demonstrations. To drive the Terrans off Shinar, we must use force.' Merdon nodded to himself. He was right, he knew, and his father wrong. And yet . . . Clanthas felt that the Komani could not be trusted. Perhaps there was a kernel of truth there.

The youth stepped away from the tri-di booth and looked around. He was in a deserted factory, one of the few that the Terrans had built before the rebellion had broken out. Long rows of silent machines stood untended in the half-light of evening. Merdon snapped off the lamp that illuminated the tri-di booth and stared briefly at the Terran machinery.

Nutrient processors. His face wrinkled in disgust at them. The Terrans can't grow food from the ground, the way

27

normal human beings do. Too slow. Not enough yield. They must hurry things, take elements directly from the soil and the air and convert them into artificial protein, synthetic foodstuffs. A few chemicals added here and a few enzymes injected there, and the accumulated knowledge of sixty centuries of planting and growing and harvesting is blasted out of existence.

He strode out of the factory, into the cool night air. Shinar had no moon, but the night-long airglow created a shimmering twilight that prevented real darkness.

Merdon looked at the youths lounging in the compound between the massive Terran buildings. These were his fighters, the new heroes of Shinar, he thought. Sons and daughters of farmers and philosophers – and even merchants.

A young girl walked up to him. 'There are some new recruits waiting to see you, on the other side of the gates.'

'Let them come in, Altai,' he said quietly.

She turned and walked toward the gate. Altai was tall for a girl, with a slim athletic build and a natural grace that made watching her a pleasure. She was not particularly beautiful, but she had the knack of looking completely feminine even in slacks, and with an automatic rifle slung over her shoulder. Maybe it was her long, jet-black hair, or her voice.

Merdon found himself smiling as he watched her go toward the gates. Maybe it was just the way she looked in slacks.

'Merdon, I have the completed tally of the weapons we got from the arsenal . . .'

He turned and focused his attention on the bookish student who had become his quartermaster. Then a half-dozen of his lieutenants converged on Merdon with questions about rations, ammunition, and the best route to take for joining up with the Komani at the valley at Carmeer.

It was nearly an hour before he could break free and inspect the new recruits. They were a typically mixed bunch: some students, a few adventurers, one boy he recognized to be a distant cousin, and a quartet of farmers, shuffling around, feeling miserably out of place.

Merdon welcomed them all solemnly.

'I want you all to realize,' he said as they gathered around him, 'that many of us will die before Shinar becomes free. If any of you are reluctant to face death, if any of you belong to families that need you to run their farms, or earn their living, you are free to go now, and no one will think less of you for it. But once you stand with us, you are in an army, and rigid discipline will be enforced.'

'May I speak?' one of the students asked.

'Certainly.'

'The ground we're standing on now was once my father's farm. The Terrans took it to build their factories.'

'What became of your father?'

'Terrans paid him what they said was a fair price for his land. He wasn't permitted to argue. He went to Kolmar City to find a job, but all he knew was farming. He . . . well, he's just a shell of the man he once was.'

'I see.'

One of the farmers spoke up. 'The same thing happened to us, in our district. I'll die before I see them turn my farm into a factory.'

The others nodded agreement.

'I hope that none of us has to die,' Merdon said quietly, 'but I expect us all to fight until we win.'

He turned the group over to one of his lieutenants and walked off toward the far end of the compound. He did not have to look over his shoulder to know that Altai was walking behind him. He slowed down and let her come abreast of him.

'You spoke to your father again?' she asked.

He nodded.

'Do the others know?'

He turned and faced her. 'What if they do? He's my father.'

She smiled. 'So touchy tonight! You get angry and argumentative every time you speak with him. Did you know that?'

'No, I didn't realize it.'

Altai put her hand to his cheek. 'You mustn't let anyone or anything upset you. Your mind must be clear at all times. You hold our lives in your hands. . . .'

'Your life too?'

'Yes.'

'And your heart?'

'Of course.'

'That's all I care about.'

She shook her head and answered gravely, 'You have much more to worry about than me.'

'I wish I didn't,' he said impulsively. He frowned for a moment, then said:

'Listen. Romal has just made up a tally of the weapons we took from the arsenal last night. I want you to divide that list in half – and tell no one except Romal about it. Then, quietly, with as few men as possible, have half the weapons stored here, and the other half sent along with the new recruits to the Komani camp tomorrow.'

'You're keeping half the weapons from the Komani?'

He nodded. 'Hide them in the buildings here. Half the ammunition, too.'

'But why?'

'I'm not sure. The Komani may be our allies, but I'd feel safer if we had some weapons available that they didn't know about. I don't want to find out some day that we've driven off the Terrans, only to have the barbarians ruling over us.'

'Suppose they discover it. . . .'

'They won't.'

'But you're supposed to go to their camp tomorrow. You'll be in their midst.'

'That's a chance I must take.'

'You're playing a dangerous game,' Altai said.

'So are we all,' Merdon replied.

CHAPTER FOUR

PRISONERS

The sun rose abruptly over the hills, and a wave of heat swept across the valley where the Mobile Force lay huddled.

Sergeant McIntyre stood before a heavy cruiser, shaking his head. 'I don't like it one bit, if you'll pardon me for saying so, sir.'

Vorgens turned to the sergeant and studied his face for a moment. It was a narrow-eyed, weather-seamed, professional soldier's face: broad and rugged, set on a thick, solid frame. McIntyre was built big, as were all the true Terrans.

'What don't you like, sergeant?' the Star Watchman asked.

'The whole setup, sir. It's goin' to take a lot more'n one heavy cruiser and a detachment of leftovers from yesterday's patrols to break through the Komani lines.'

'Would you rather report back to your company commander?'

McIntyre's eyes widened in surprise for just a flash of a second. Then he drew himself up as straight as he could stand. 'No sir. I was asked to volunteer and I did. I'll stick it out as long as you do, sir.'

Vorgens smiled. 'Good. I don't like the setup any more than you do, sergeant, but somebody's got to try it, and I guess we've been nominated. Let's start moving.'

They swung up the ladder and ducked into the turret hatch. The cruiser was air-conditioned to Terran standards; the sudden drop of temperature inside made Vorgens shudder involuntarily. He felt more comfortable in the hot sunshine.

The cruiser's blowers whined shrilly and blasted jets of air straight downward. As the shrieking grew higher in pitch, the lumbering behemoth edged higher off the ground, while the air jets scoured dust and rocks from beneath it. Finally the turbos' whining rose past the range audible to the human ear; the cruiser was now a good foot above the ground.

31

She slid forward slowly, hatches open and a knot of foot-soldiers riding topside behind the turret.

When they reached the end of the valley floor and rumbled past the last perimeter entrenchment, Vorgens popped out of the turret hatch and told the footmen:

'All right, now – get off and spread out. Keep low and move fast. Stay within sight of the cruiser. Report the slightest sign of movement. Remember, they've been watching us from up in the hills, so we're bound to be attacked.'

He dropped back into the bowels of the cruiser and strapped himself into a slightly too-big bucket seat, next to McIntyre. Vorgens turned on the omnidirectional video scanner and donned the communications headset.

Soon they were climbing the first low hills, and the countryside was changing from the bare rockiness of the valley to wide patches of dark grass and ever-thickening bush.

'These cruisers ain't much help in this terrain,' McIntyre muttered.

'What's that?' Vorgens asked.

'Cruisers can't take a very steep grade, sir. In climbing terrain like this, we've gotta stick to the gentlest slopes. That means the Komani can plot our course before we can. They know just where we've gotta go.'

'Hm. Perhaps so.' Vorgens fingered the control dials of the scanner. 'No sign of anything so far, though.'

After a few minutes of silence, McIntyre said, 'Sir?'

'Yes?' Vorgens answered without taking his eyes from the screen.

'How come a Star Watch officer is leadin' this mission? If you don't mind my asking, sir.'

Vorgens looked up at him. 'Brigadier Aikens is in charge of all Imperial personnel on this planet.'

'But ain't the Imperial Marines under the Star Watch's command? I mean, the Marines – this Mobile Force – we're just a branch of the Star Watch.'

Vorgens nodded. 'Yes. Brigadier Aikens takes orders from the Star Watch High Command. That doesn't mean that a Star Watch junior officer can order around a full brigadier. You know that, sergeant. What are you driving at?'

'Maybe I shouldn't be repeating a rumor, sir,' McIntyre

said, avoiding Vorgens' eyes, 'but – well, is it true that you were supposed to arrange a truce with the Komani?'

So he knows! Vorgens thought. *Probably the word is out to every trooper in the Mobile Force.*

Aloud, he answered, 'I was ordered to arrange a truce, when the military situation permits negotiations to be made. Brigadier Aikens must decide when the situation is right for truce talks. I'm responsible to him while I'm here.'

'And he ordered you on this breakout mission,' McIntyre said.

'Yes.'

'That means he don't want a truce . . . and he don't expect us back. He's gonna fight the Komani, and he wants us – you, that is – out of his way.'

Vorgens stiffened. 'Sergeant, our mission is to break through the Komani lines and summon reinforcements to the Mobile Force, not to make half-cocked psychoanalyses of our commanding officer.' *No matter how right they may be,* he added silently.

'Yes sir,' McIntyre said.

The ground got steeper and more densely covered with foliage as the hours passed. As McIntyre had predicted, the cruiser's pilot had to keep the vehicle gliding along the flattest, easiest slopes. They followed a twisting, meandering path, avoiding the steeper grades and areas that were covered with boulders or large bushes. The sun climbed higher as Vorgens silently watched the seemingly empty countryside unfold on his scanner screen.

There are a thousand places for an ambush along this way, he thought. *But it will take some doing for even Komani warriors to stop a heavy cruiser. It all depends on what kinds of weapons they have; how much equipment. Like the tales of the old ones back home, when the Terrans first proclaimed their Empire . . . men against machines.*

'Enemy breastworks at ten o'clock!'

Vorgens snapped his attention to the viewscreen. He twisted a dial and saw the entrenchment, about a hundred-fifty yards from the cruiser. He dialed a close-up view. Empty.

'Hey, they're firing from the ridge – three o'clock!' another footman called.

Vorgens dialed the scene. Sporadic small-arms fire was coming from the ridge. Off to one side, he noticed a small clump of trees. He dialed a close-up.

'Enemy troops in those trees at two o'clock,' he called into his mouthpiece.

The footmen on the right flank dropped to the ground as McIntyre drove the turret around and swept the trees with ultrasonic beams. Then he swung back and launched a missile toward the ridge.

'They're charging! Ten o'clock!'

Komani warriors were swarming in on one-man flyers, saddlelike machines that gave them terrifying speed and mobility. Vorgens could see them plainly now, huge, humanoid warriors in gleaming battle armor, their arms covered with fuzzy greenish hair, their faces more like cats than men.

McIntyre was blazing away with everything available now and the footmen were laying down a heavy fire. The Komani were being mown down in the volley, but still more of them came, some of them brandishing their ceremonial broadswords.

Vorgens dialed the other side of the cruiser, and spoke into his mouthpiece, 'Keep both our flanks covered, no matter . . .'

The screen exploded in a shower of glass and Vorgens was smashed back in his chair as the whole cruiser lurched violently.

Vorgens shook his head groggily. It was dark inside the turret, and strangely quiet. A surge of panic flashed through the Watchman, but he fought it down automatically. The cruiser was stopped. Power off. *But I'm still in one piece . . . I think.*

Vorgens unbuckled his safety strap and turned around in his seat. His head hurt, a dull, sullen pain. In the dimness he could see McIntyre sprawled unconscious next to him, his left arm twisted grotesquely.

Unconscious or – no, no – he's breathing.

His eyes were getting accustomed to the shadows now. Vorgens could both see and smell a faint acrid smoke drifting through the shattered turret. There were no signs of life from the men below. He realized that his right hand was throbbing. A glass splinter was sticking into the palm and a steady trickle of blood oozed from it.

He pulled it out, wincing, then reached across McIntyre's inert form for the first-aid kit on the turret bulkhead. Clumsily, with his left hand, he swabbed the cut and sprayed a plastic over it. Then he carefully brushed his jacket and pants clean of the other fragments that had showered him.

McIntyre began to moan.

'Easy sergeant. Don't try to move. Your arm's broken.'

'What happened?'

'Nuclear grenade, I imagine. They only needed one.'

McIntyre closed his eyes and leaned back. 'I told you we weren't supposed to come out of this alive.'

'We're not dead yet.'

Vorgens rose from his seat gingerly. His knees were a little wobbly, but only a little. He jabbed a sedative into McIntyre's good arm, then decided it was too cramped and dark in the turret to attempt to set the broken bone. He reached up for the overhead hatch, the debris littering the deck crunching under his boots as he moved.

'I'm going to take a look around,' he said to McIntyre.

The Watchman climbed up on his chair and pushed open the turret hatch. Cautiously he stuck his head out into the sunshine. The right side of the cruiser was smashed in, the turret itself tilted slightly askew. For a radius of fifty yards around, the ground was scorched black.

At the top of a little hillock, some hundred yards from the cruiser, three figures were moving slowly among the sprawled bodies. Two were Komani warriors, the third a native of Oran VI who wore the flowing white robes of a priest.

Blessing the dead, Vorgens thought.

They saw him, and one of the warriors raised his rifle.

'Don't fire!' Vorgens called out in standard Terran. 'There's a wounded man in here.'

'Bring him out,' the warrior commanded.

'I'll need help.'

They consulted among themselves. The warriors seemed apathetic, but the olive-skinned priest evidently persuaded them. One of the Komani came while the other remained with the priest, armed and ready. The warrior literally

35

dwarfed Vorgens. His powerful body looked fully human, but his face was feline – wide-spaced cat's eyes, flat nose, broad slash of a mouth. His ears were a pair of tiny cups atop his skull. The whole face and head was covered with a wiry, greenish fuzz.

With the giant Komani's help, Vorgens pulled McIntyre out of the turret and carried him to the shade of the trees atop the hillock. The native priest set the sergeant's arm while Vorgens applied Terran anesthetics and antibiotics. Together, they put on a plastic splint and binding.

'Are we the only ones left alive?' Vorgens asked the priest in his own language after McIntyre was safely asleep.

'About half the Komani force survived. They have gone elsewhere now, leaving only these two to search for loot and prisoners. There are two others of your footmen nearby, although one is near death from his wounds.'

The priest led Vorgens across to the windswept ridge on the other side of the cruiser. They both tried for more than an hour to save the wounded trooper – in vain. Then they started back to the grove of trees where McIntyre was resting. With them came the other Terran prisoner – Private Neal Giradaux – tall, lanky, trying hard not to look afraid.

'You speak our tongue,' the priest observed as they walked back to the trees.

'It was taught to me before I was sent here,' Vorgens said. 'Actually, it's not much different from my own native language.'

By the time they got back to the grove, McIntyre was sitting up with his back against a tree, his splinted and band-aged left arm sticking out awkwardly at his side. The two Komani warriors stood some distance away, aloof and impassive.

'By glory, it's Mac!' Giradaux shouted as they approached. 'You're alive, sarge!'

'Well, if you made it, soldier,' McIntyre shot back, 'did you think I wouldn't?'

Giradaux ran up to the sergeant and squatted beside him. 'Are you okay, Sarge?'

'Broke my arm when they got the cruiser. How about you?'

36

'Knocked out by the blast. That's all.'

Vorgens joined them as the priest went to the two warriors. 'You two are in the same outfit?'

'Not now sir,' McIntyre answered. 'But I broke this pup into the service a coupla years ago.'

'I see,' Vorgens said. 'Sergeant, do you feel strong enough to walk? The priest tells me that the Komani want to take us to their headquarters.'

McIntyre grunted. 'I guess I'll hafta walk, then ... or be dragged.'

'I'll help you, Sarge,' Giradaux offered.

'Get your trench-diggin' hands off me!' McIntyre bellowed. 'You think a busted arm means I'm helpless?'

'No, Sarge.' Giradaux grinned.

McIntyre struggled to his feet and stood at attention. 'All right, sir. I'm ready to go.'

The sun was nearly at zenith as the little band of men started their journey. The beginning was easy enough – down the reverse slope of the hills they had been in most of the morning. The sun's warmth was tempered by cool breezes and frequent clumps of trees that threw dense shade. They stopped briefly after an hour's march and ate a scant meal: a few dried vegetables, a lump of something like bread, and water from a running stream.

Then came the worst of it – trudging across another dry, rocky valley under the heat of the afternoon sun.

The yellow sun seemed to hang directly overhead, no matter how far or how long they plodded across the barren valley. Twice the size of Sol and six times brighter, Oran beat mercilessly on the bare rocks, withering the scrubby plants, making the air dance with heat currents, wringing streams of sweat from the weary men, roaring in their ears and dazzling their eyes with painful glare.

McIntyre had pulled down the glare visor from his helmet when they started across the valley. But as they struggled through the long afternoon, he saw that Vorgens and Giradaux had neither helmet nor visor.

'Sir,' he asked of Vorgens, 'would you like my helmet?'

The Star Watchman shook his head. 'No thanks, Sergeant.'

'I have an extra pair of glare goggles in my pocket, then.

37

They're on this side,' he gestured with his bandaged arm, 'so you'll hafta get them for yourself.'

'I don't need them, McIntyre, thanks. This star is pretty bright, but it's not as brilliant as the one I was born under. What I need more than goggles is a long, cool drink and a fresh breeze.'

McIntyre was silent for a moment.

'You might give the goggles to Giradaux. He seems to be having a hard time of it.'

McIntyre grinned. 'Yes sir. Hey, Gerry!' he called to the trooper, marching a few yards ahead of them.

'Yeah, Sarge?'

'Where's your helmet, trooper?'

Giradaux slackened his pace momentarily, until he was beside the other two. 'Gee, Sarge, I dunno where it is. I must've left it on that ridge . . .'

McIntyre shook his head. 'You're expected to give up your weapon when you're taken prisoner, but you don't hafta strip naked! That helmet costs the Empire money.'

'I know, Sarge,' Giradaux looked miserable, 'and I could use the glare visor, too.'

'Here, fish in this pocket and get my spare goggles before you go blind . . .'

'Thanks, Mac!'

'Think I'm gonna let you charge the Empire for a disability pension because you're careless?'

The going got rougher as the long afternoon wore on. Before they reached high ground again, McIntyre was allowing Giradaux and Vorgens to take turns supporting him. The priest gave them water from a canteen he carried within the folds of his robe. The Komani warriors were impassive, except for insisting that the prisoners maintain the pace of the march.

'How come the Komani don't need glare visors?' Giradaux asked as they struggled up a slope.

'Look at their eyes,' McIntyre answered. 'They narrow down to slits . . . just like a rotten cat's.'

Finally they reached the crest of a wooded ridge, and were out of the glaring heat. They rested for a few minutes, then were on their way again – this time along the ridge, under the tall trees.

With McIntyre able to get along by himself again, Vorgens turned his attention to the surroundings. The trees, the grass, the blue sky, the sounds of birds and insects . . . it was practically the same as on his homeworld. The leaves were a darker shade of green, the birds were slightly different . . . yet not so different after all. And the native priest – he was smaller than Vorgens, his skin slightly darker. No doubt his bones and joints and internal organs were somewhat different, but he was human. ·

Thousands of parsecs from his homeworld, and even farther from Earth, here was a planet that bore not only Earth-type life, but human life.

Don't get emotional, Vorgens told himself. *Human life is a logical development in the evolution of an Earth-type planet. It happened on your homeworld, it happened on Earth, it's happened spontaneously on some fifteen thousand planets within the Empire.*

He watched a small, furry animal scurry across the trail up ahead and dash up a tree trunk. *Still,* he thought, *it's not much less than miraculous.*

The priest especially fascinated Vorgens. He was evidently quite old, yet he carried himself with a dignity that forced respect. His skin was a deep brown, his eyes jet black, and what was left of his wispy hair was silverish. His face was spiderwebbed with age, and Vorgens finally realized that this was what intrigued him. He had never seen a really old person before, not face to face. On Plione IX, his homeworld, on Mars, where he received his Star Watch training, on Earth and throughout the Terran Empire, he had never seen a truly old person close up. The physical signs of age had been eliminated by Terran science centuries ago.

Vorgens soon found himself talking with the priest – Sittas was his name – as the little group made its way through the cool woods. They talked of general things, noncommittal things, things that had nothing to do with war and the inevitability of death.

'Tell me of your homeworld,' Sittas asked.

'It's a long, long distance from here, even in a starship,' Vorgens said. 'Plione IX – the ninth planet circling the star that the Terrans call Plione; a giant blue star, much larger and hotter than Oran, although our planet is considerably farther away from Plione than you are from your sun.'

'And your homeworld is like our world here?'

Vorgens nodded. 'Very much. It's a little smaller than Oran VI . . .'

'What is Oran VI?'

'Huh? Why, this planet – your world, here.'

'Of course, of course,' Sittas said, smiling. 'That is the Terran name for our world. In the hill villages, where I am from, we see very few Terrans.'

'What do you call the planet?'

'Its name is Shinar.'

'Shinar,' Vorgens repeated. 'That means . . . um, something to do with home, isn't it?'

The priest nodded. 'Home, yes. It also means peace, and life, and many other things besides.'

They walked in silence for a few minutes. Then Vorgens said, 'I'm surprised to see a native priest with the Komani raiders.'

Sittas smiled. 'They have souls. I am a priest.'

'Yes, but they are looting your people – turning your planet into a battlefield . . .'

'Does that make them impossible to change? Does that doom them to our everlasting hatred? Were not the Komani of this very clan once the allies of the Terrans?'

'Yes,' Vorgens admitted. 'The entire Komani nation fought on the side of the Terrans in the Galactic War, but that was a century ago, and now . . .'

'And now you kill one another. Does that mean that you cannot stop the killing and live in peace once again?'

'I see,' Vorgens said. 'I understand.' To himself he added, *We have a lot in common, old man. You and I may be the only sane ones on this planet.*

Sittas changed the subject abruptly, and the young Star Watchman told the old priest of many things as they walked through the long afternoon under the cool trees along the nameless ridge. Vorgens found himself talking for the first time in years about his homeworld.

Plione IX, circling the brightest star of the Pleiades, a massive blue giant whose fierce radiation made life impossible on all but its outermost planets.

Plione IX, known as *Bhr'houd'grinr* until the Terrans landed and began to homogenize the local culture into the standard Terran blend and incorporate the planet into the efficient, expanding Empire.

'My people were also allies of the Terrans during the Galactic War,' Vorgens said, 'but when we were annexed into the Empire, instead of allowed our own government, the people tried to fight. It was hopeless, though.

'My grandfather was one of the few men on our planet to recognize that the Terrans were unbeatable,' Vorgens told the receptive Sittas. 'As proof of his convictions, he sent his oldest son to join the Terran Star Watch, to be trained and educated by the Terrans – to serve them. By this example, he hoped to prove to his compatriots that life within the Terran Empire was better than a hopeless war of resistance.'

'And was he successful?' Sittas asked.

Vorgens shrugged. 'He died before the war was finally ended. Assassinated. Plione IX is now a peaceful member of the Empire; its people are prosperous and happy. My father is still in the Star Watch, and he made certain that I became a Watchman, too.'

'And you?'

'I'm not very prosperous,' Vorgens answered, smiling, 'but I was happy enough in the Star Watch – until Oran VI. I mean, Shinar.'

Then, quite suddenly, Vorgens had nothing left to say to the priest. They had talked of the past and the present, but neither of them wanted to speak about the future. They moved apart by mutual, unspoken agreement.

Vorgens rejoined McIntyre and Giradaux, who were still slogging along side by side over the steadily-rising ground.

'How's it going?' Vorgens asked the sergeant.

McIntyre shrugged with one shoulder. 'Okay. The arm hurts a little, but not much. You know, we've been passin' guard posts for the past hour or so.'

'I hadn't noticed,' Vorgens blurted.

McIntyre pointed with his eyes. 'Up there, sir, there's another one.'

Vorgens glanced at a jutting rock off to one side of the trail. A Komani was flattened out on top of it, his greenish body hair and gray clothing a near-perfect camouflage in the heavy foliage atop the rock.

'Yes, I see,' Vorgens said. 'We must be approaching their headquarters.'

'Gerry and I have been takin' bearings as well as we can, sir,' McIntyre said in a lower voice. 'I think we'll be able to spot their headquarters on map co-ordinates when we get back to the Mobile Force.'

'Fine,' Vorgens said absently as he silently changed McIntyre's *when* to an *if*.

'Sir?' Giradaux asked, and at Vorgens' nod went on, 'How come a native priest is with the Komani? I thought the barbarians were raiding this planet and the natives want us to throw 'em out.'

'That's what I thought, too,' Vorgens said. 'But there's more to this story than the part we know. A lot more.'

CHAPTER FIVE

THE FACE OF THE ENEMY

The Komani camp was a shock.

Not only was it bigger and much better equipped than Vorgens had expected, but there were almost as many Shinarian natives milling around in it as Komani.

The camp was set on a broad, thinly wooded meadow. Off to one end were dozens of landing ships, slim, needle-nosed, erect and gleaming in the slanting rays of the setting sun. Except for a small blast ring around the ships, the meadow was covered with Komani bubble-tents, thousands of them, each brightly colored in a distinctive family insignia, each housing anywhere from one warrior to a dozen. Laced between the colorful bubbles were pennants, ceremonial fires, stacks of equipment and weapons.

The exact center of the encampment was the site of the largest tent of all, colored pure gold: the home of the tribal Kang.

'They're pretty brazen, camping in the open,' McIntyre growled as they first saw the meadow.

'They've probably got an energy screen that'll protect 'em against missiles and aircraft, Sarge,' Giradaux said. 'You'd either have to hit 'em with heavy beamguns from a starship, or attack 'em overland. They've got the approaches bottled up pretty tight.'

McIntyre muttered to himself.

They were led into the camp, through row after row of gaudy bubble-tents, stared at silently by the solemn Komani warriors, women and children. They stared back intently at this unexpected close-up of their enemy's base.

'What're all the natives doin' here?' McIntyre wondered. 'I thought the Komani were raidin' them. Why're they actin' so friendly?'

The Shinarians were there, if not in force, then certainly in numbers. Groups of olive-skinned natives were everywhere in the Komani camp, selling food to Komani women, bargaining over jewelry with Komani nobles, demonstrating mobile energy beam projectors to Komani technicians.

But, worse still, Vorgens saw many of the natives were simply talking – quietly and earnestly – with Komani warriors. And the natives wore weapons.

Finally the Terrans were ushered into a bubble-tent. It was furnished with a single low-slung table; nothing else. The lone doorway was guarded by four heavily armed warriors, the smallest of them a full head taller and seemingly a yard wider than McIntyre.

'The last word in hospitality,' Giradaux joked lamely.

McIntyre tapped a heel on the floor of the tent. 'Plasti-steel, I bet. We won't be diggin' our way out.'

'No, we're here to stay,' Vorgens admitted, 'for awhile.'

The last shafts of sunlight were disappearing behind the forest at the edge of the meadow when a Komani youth arrived at the entrance with a tray of food. The youngster hesitated momentarily at the doorway, then walked in, very stiff and grave, placed the tray on the bare table, and half-ran out of the tent.

'Guess he thought we'd eat *him*,' McIntyre said.

It was a good enough meal, although less than would satisfy the Terrans' appetites. By the time they finished eating it was dark. The night-long twilight of Shinar was broken only by the ceremonial campfires that dotted the camp.

McIntyre rose from his cross-legged squat at the table, stretched as well as he could with his bandaged arm, and said, 'I'm gonna grab some sack time. With your permission, sir.'

'It's not my permission that counts,' Vorgens murmured.

'Sir?'

'Nothing, sergeant. Go on, have a good sleep. We can skip the formalities for the time being.'

'Okay, sir. If you want me, just holler.'

With a nod of his head, McIntyre made it clear to Giradaux that he should sleep, too.

Vorgens left them alone and stepped out to the doorway of the tent. He could sense the Komani guards tighten a fraction as he appeared in the flickering firelight. He stopped just outside the doorway. The guards said nothing.

Vorgens stood there looking out across the bizarre camp,

44

etched in firelight. A chilling night breeze moaned by, and then, mixed with it, came a low, plaintive chant from somewhere near the center of the meadow.

He listened as the slow, melancholy sound of women's voices drifted through the night. *A funeral dirge*, he realized finally. *A dirge for the men who were killed today. For the men we killed today.*

The Star Watchman remained motionless as he listened to the weird, haunting music. But his mind was churning endlessly and again he saw the charging Komani warriors, heard the shouted orders, the blasts of weapons, the screams of men in battle. Now he realized that these warriors – these men – were also sons and fathers who feared death as much as anyone. What was it the old priest had said? *They have souls.*

The dirge ended at last, and one of the campfires suddenly blazed into a huge pyre. Vorgens watched as the flames soared skyward and then, slowly, slowly, died down into nothingness. After the funeral pyre had faded completely, Vorgens found himself looking up at the stars overhead. The airglow and the glare of the campfires made it impossible to see any but the nearest, brightest stars. Vorgens knew that the Pleiades were too far away to be seen, and then he realized, with a sudden shock, that he did not even know just where in the skies of Shinar they would appear.

'Can you see your home star?'

Vorgens turned to find Sittas standing beside him. 'No,' he answered. 'I don't even know where to look for it.'

'Are your men comfortable?'

'They've eaten and now they're asleep.'

Sittas nodded. 'Would you like to talk? I have many questions on my mind. Or perhaps you are tired from today's – events.'

'No, I couldn't sleep if I tried. I have some questions, too.'

'Good, we can talk.' The old priest turned to the guards and said a few words to them in their own language, then led Vorgens away from the tent.

'I find that walking stimulates my conversation,' Sittas said. 'Walking and conversation are the only vices left to one of my age.'

Vorgens studied the old man's face in the flickering firelight. On another world, at another time, Sittas might have been a teacher, or a physician, or even a planetary governor. His face had the natural dignity, the touch of good humor at the corners of the mouth, the impression of wisdom in the silver hair and wrinkled brow. But deep in his eyes was a sadness born of many years and long experience of the failure of man's grandest dreams.

'I was surprised,' Vorgens said finally, 'to see so many Shinarians in camp.'

Sittas said nothing.

'I had thought . . . that is, Terran intelligence believes, that the Komani raiders have landed on your planet while you are in rebellion against the Empire – taking advantage of the confused situation to loot your people.'

'There *was* some looting,' Sittas agreed noncommittally.

'I don't understand.'

Sittas stopped walking and looked up at the young Watchman. 'Perhaps it is not me you should speak with, but Merdon.'

'Who is Merdon?'

'A youth – very much like yourself. And yet, very unlike you.'

Vorgens shrugged. 'All right, let's talk to Merdon.'

Sittas led him through a maze of tents, and finally left him standing in front of one of the smaller bubbles. After a few minutes, the old priest reappeared at the doorway and gestured Vorgens inside.

The tent was sparsely furnished with three cots, a table, a pair of chests, a few stools, and a single globular lamp overhead. Seated behind the table was Merdon, poring over a big paper map and a pile of reports; a miniature tri-di transceiver held down one corner of the map, and a beam pistol rested on the opposite corner.

Merdon looked up as Sittas said, 'This is the Star Watchman I told you about.'

'*Vhro'rgyns* is my name. The Terrans find it easier to say Vorgens.'

Merdon looked into the Watchman's tawny eyes and smiled. 'In this case, I find myself forced to agree with the Terrans. I am Merdon – in Terran as well as Shinarian.'

46

Merdon gestured to the stools before the table, and Vorgens and Sittas sat down.

'Sittas tells me,' Merdon said, 'that you can't understand why so many Shinarians are here in the Komani encampment. The answer is simple: the Komani are here in Shinar because we invited them here. They are our guests, our allies. They are helping us to fight against the Terrans.'

Vorgens felt his breath catch in amazement. 'You . . . *invited* the Komani? As mercenary troops?'

'As allies. Oh, I know what the Terran commanders think. They believe that we on Shinar are acting as unwitting pawns for some deep, dark Komani plan of conquest. The truth is exactly the opposite. The Komani are working for us.'

'Why?'

Merdon snapped, 'Why? Why do you think? Because we want to be rid of the Terrans and their blasted Empire!'

'But why should the Komani help you? What do they gain by going against the Empire?'

Merdon's brows knitted thoughtfully for a moment. Then he replied, 'The Komani are born fighters. The smell of battle, a chance of loot – that's all they want.'

'You make it sound very simple,' Vorgens said quietly.

'No, it's the Terrans who oversimplify everything. They think that because our culture is a peaceful, agricultural society that we are a simple, stupid people. That is a mistake. We are as complex in our desires, in our fears, in our loves and hates, as any Terran – or any other human.'

'All right,' Vorgens agreed, 'but what's that got to do with—'

'Your Terran officials think that we Shinarians are all sheep. Well, perhaps many of us are. But not all of us.'

'So you decided to resist the Empire.'

'A few of us did, yes. Some tried to resist with words, with protests, with street demonstrations. The Terrans' answer was force. Well, now we are meeting force with force. We will fight and die and fight again until the Terrans are no longer willing to pay the price for Shinar. Until they leave us in freedom.'

'And the Komani are helping you in this struggle.'

47

'The Komani – and any other recruits we can find,' Merdon said, looking straight at Vorgens.

'Any other recruits?' the Watchman echoed.

Merdon leaned across the table. 'You are not a Terran. Sittas tells me that your own people fought against the Empire. Join us! Help us to free Shinar! Perhaps someday we can destroy this evil Empire altogether, and free your own people.'

Vorgens blinked, and turned toward Sittas. The priest shrugged his bony shoulders to indicate that the idea was Merdon's alone.

'I am not a native Terran, that is true,' Vorgens said, 'but I am a citizen of the Empire. My people did fight against the Terrans, once, a long time ago. But today they are so much a part of the Empire that they could not establish an independent nation if they wanted to – which they don't. I am a sworn officer of the Star Watch. I cannot turn my back on my own word, and fight against the men with whom I have served.'

'You hide behind your duty,' Merdon snapped.

Vorgens' face tightened. 'Perhaps so. But listen to me. No matter what the Empire has done on Shinar, the peoples ruled by the Terrans would be plunged into chaos and starvation if the Empire were destroyed. The Terrans may seem evil and arbitrary to you – perhaps they are, in many cases – but they are also the carriers of law, of stability, of commerce and order, throughout more than half the galaxy. Their job is not an easy one. Here on Shinar they may have failed, but you cannot destroy the Empire unless you replace it with something better . . . not unless you are an unthinking barbarian, as the Komani are.'

'You *are* a Terran, after all,' Merdon growled.

'I am an officer of the Star Watch,' Vorgens said, his voice rising. 'I was sent to Shinar to try to arrange a truce that will end this bloodshed. I can offer you the same terms I offer the Komani: lay down your arms and return to your homes. Otherwise the Empire will be forced to crush you.'

'Get out!' Merdon shouted. 'Take your truce terms and go back to your tent and wait for the Komani to deal with you. Star Watchman, truce-bearer – you're a prisoner, a Komani prisoner, and before long you'll be dead!'

Vorgens rose and strode from the tent. Sittas hurried out after him.

'He had no excuse for speaking to you like that,' the priest said. 'I am ashamed for him.'

'He lost his temper,' Vorgens said, calmer now in the open air. 'I know I lost mine. We see the world through different eyes . . . And he's right, you know. I am a prisoner. I'm not in a position to offer anyone anything.'

'Still, Merdon's behavior was inexcusable.'

'He just doesn't understand the reason for the Empire.'

'I must confess,' Sittas said softly, 'that I, myself, do not see why the Empire must have this particular planet, when there are so many . . .'

Vorgens thought it over for a moment, then answered, 'I suppose the answer is that, if Shinar were allowed to quit the Empire, others would want to leave it, also. It's the first step on the road to chaos.

'The Terrans didn't want an Empire. No one planned it this way. At one moment, the Terran Confederation was fighting for its life against the Masters. A moment later, the Masters were utterly defeated, and their empire fell to the Terrans. Suddenly the Terrans found themselves responsible for administering, feeding, governing, half the galaxy. They tried to get various star systems to govern themselves, but it didn't work out. The Empire was needed. The Terrans had no choice.'

'Regardless of the cost,' Sittas said.

'The cost?'

'Yes. In maintaining the Empire of the Masters and making it their own, the Terrans have obliterated the individual cultures of their member planets. Their effort to turn Shinar into a Terran-type food-manufacturing world has touched off this war. You, yourself, told me how your native culture has been submerged by the Terrans.'

Vorgens nodded. 'That's right. My people are almost exactly like all the other people in the Empire. The old customs, the old beliefs – they're only for teachers of ancient history, or museum keepers. I – I suppose it was inevitable. Unavoidable.'

'Was it?' Sittas asked.

'Yes,' Vorgens replied. 'There are reasons . . .'

'Reasons?'

Vorgens looked at the old priest for a long moment. Then he began to explain to him what every servant of the Empire was expressly forbidden to tell a native.

He told Sittas of the Terrans' gradual realization that, a million years earlier, a race of Terrans had reached into space, met a powerful alien race, and been smashed in a devastating war. He told the priest of the discovery of the ruins on Mars, of the machinery that had produced the Ice Ages that was found on Titan, of the remnants of the crumbled First Empire that the Terrans had found as they expanded into the stars once again.

'They are building their new Empire as solidly as they can,' Vorgens finished, 'because they know that somewhere among the stars – perhaps in another galaxy, even – the Others still exist. They nearly exterminated the Terrans once, a million years ago. The Terrans are building an Empire that can exterminate the Others, if they show up again.'

'And for this reason Shinar must become a cog in their Imperial machine?'

Vorgens nodded.

'Are we not men? Would we not help to fight the Others?'

'I know,' the Star Watchman said. 'My own people would, too. They wouldn't have to be regimented by the Terrans. But now my homeworld is a planet of mines and factories. There are ten times more people there than we could possibly feed with our own resources. If, for some reason, the Empire should break down, nine people of every ten would starve.'

'Yet you fight for the Terrans.'

Vorgens shrugged. 'I fight for what I believe. The Empire is not the best way, but it's the only way we have. Its laws are just. I know that what's happening to your planet is hard to accept, but there is no alternative. I don't like to fight against your people, but your people started the fighting.'

Sittas agreed with a nod. 'Yet, who is without blame in a war?'

'It's no longer a matter of blame,' Vorgens said. 'Now we must decide where we go from here.'

They found themselves back at Vorgens' tent, with its quadruple guard.

'You have answered my questions quite frankly,' Sittas said, 'for which I thank you. Now tell me, what questions can I answer for you?'

Vorgens immediately asked. 'How many Komani warriors are on Shinar?'

'I don't really know,' the priest said. 'An entire clan has landed here, as you can see. I suppose there must be something like fifteen thousand fighting men.'

'An entire clan,' Vorgens repeated. 'And who is their chief?'

'Okatar Kang.'

'Could you arrange an audience with him for me? Tomorrow, as early as possible?'

Sittas shook his head. 'That I cannot do. The Kang does not usually see prisoners, unless they are remarkable in some respect – a general, or a renowned warrior. I have no influence whatsoever over Okatar and his Elders. Merdon might have arranged such a meeting, but . . .' Sittas's voice trailed off.

'I see,' Vorgens said. 'Well, thank you anyway. I'm sorry the meeting with Merdon wasn't more fruitful.'

Sittas nodded silently.

'Good night,' Vorgens said.

'Good fortune to you, my friend.'

Vorgens watched the old man disappear among the tents, and slowly realized that it was the first time since he had left the Star Watch Academy that someone had called him 'friend'.

Inside the tent, he found McIntyre and Giradaux awake, talking quietly while squatting as far from the entrance – and the guards – as they could.

Vorgens told them what he had learned from Sittas.

'So it seems that we are facing not just the Komani,' he concluded, 'but a well-armed and very determined band of rebels, as well.'

'It's a dirty business,' McIntyre grumbled. 'Fighting these barbarians is bad enough, but half the planet might be up in arms against us.'

Vorgens nodded. 'Under any circumstances, it means that the forces holding down the Mobile Force could be two or even three times larger than Brigadier Aikens believes them to be.'

'We've gotta get back to the Force tonight,' McIntyre said, 'and let them know what they're up against.'

'Right,' Vorgens said.

'The Sarge and I were talking over our chances of breaking outta here,' Giradaux said.

'And?'

McIntyre answered, 'There's four guards against the three of us. They're armed. Gerry was frisked good when they captured him. He's clean. I managed to sneak a stinger under my belt before they took us.' He pulled out a slim rod. 'It won't kill anybody, but it'll put him outta commission for a few hours.'

Vorgens grinned. 'Good. And I fixed that cast of yours so that it ought to be as hard as plastisteel by now.'

McIntyre looked surprised. He tapped the cast on the floor. It sounded good. He ran a hand over the innocent-looking bandages. 'By Pluto, this'll break any bone in the galaxy. Did you bring anything from the cruiser, sir?'

'Just something from the medical kit. It's not a weapon, but it could be just as important to us.'

He pulled a small bottle of pills from his jacket pocket. 'These are mescal capsules,' Vorgens explained, opening the bottle and handing them out. 'They speed up your perceptions, temporarily, so that everything around you seems to be moving very slowly. If we're going to depend on surprise, it might be useful to be able to see the enemy's reactions in slow motion. It would give you time to think about your next move – in the middle of a hand-to-hand fight!'

McIntyre popped a capsule into his mouth, swallowed hard, then grinned. 'I'm glad we've got a Star Watchman with us, sir. Us poor footsloggers wouldn't think to look for weapons in the infirmary.'

'Coming from you, sergeant, that's a real compliment.'

They discussed tactics for a few minutes, while allowing the mescal to take effect. As a test, Vorgens took McIntyre's stinger and dropped it to the floor. It floated down like a feather and bounced lazily for what seemed like several minutes. They were ready.

Their plan was simple, based on speed and surprise.

Giradaux was lead man. He came bombing out of the tent at top speed, diving straight into one of the guards. The big Komani, half asleep, toppled over and Giradaux started to spin free of him. As the other three guards turned to face the Terran, drawing their weapons, Vorgens and McIntyre entered the fight.

It all seemed like a dream to Vorgens, under the effect of the mescal. Every move they made – friend and foe alike – had that underwater languor about it. He saw the Komani drawing their sidearms, saw Gerry slowly rising to his feet.

Then the nearest Komani began to turn toward him. Vorgens raised the stinger (it seemed an eternity to lift it) and touched it to the warrior's chest. He froze for an instant, then began slumping toward the ground.

Vorgens turned to see McIntyre swinging his arm-cast into the face of a startled Komani. Another was already on the way down, his head split and bleeding. Giradaux chopped artfully at the neck of the warrior he had toppled, and the fight was abruptly finished. Vorgens' stunned victim finally hit the ground, as if to punctuate the end of it.

They took the Komani sidearms and made a cautious retreat to the edge of the camp. It was late, and the camp was quiet. No one seemed to be stirring.

Vorgens whispered an order to set the captured handguns to stun, rather than on killing power. McIntyre grumbled something about 'fighting tomorrow the enemies we don't kill tonight,' but a quick glance at the Star Watchman showed that he was not going to argue the point.

Their first trouble came at the outer guard perimeter. A Komani warrior spotted them and let out a warning yelp before McIntyre's shot knocked him unconscious.

Then it was an agonizing race in slow motion for the edge of the meadow. Beacon flares began to pop around them, and although Vorgens knew that the three of them were dashing for the thick foliage at the meadow's edge, the mescal made it seem as though they were suspended in midflight while the whole Komani camp had plenty of time to take leisurely aim at them.

53

'They ain't set to stun!' McIntyre yelled as energy beams sizzled past them.

They zigzagged the last few yards to the meadow's edge and plunged down the steep slope, stumbling and falling in the darkness. They made their way toward the thick brush, where they would be safe from the Komani – temporarily.

After a few minutes' thrashing through the foliage, they found a gulley that led away from the camp. They flopped down, bellies in the dirt, and gasped for breath.

'Everyone okay?' Vorgens asked.

Two grunts answered him. Through the foliage, he could see lights swinging back and forth.

'Sergeant, can you find your way back to the Mobile Force from here?'

'I think so, sir.' McIntyre said.

'Can you evade those guard posts we saw on the way up here?'

'Yes sir.'

They could hear shouts now, and the sounds of men probing through the brush.

'All right, sergeant,' Vorgens said. 'You and Giradaux make a break for it. I'll scuttle off in another direction, making enough noise for the Komani to spot me. I'll lead them on as long as I can. You two make certain to get back to Brigadier Aikens.'

'But, sir . . .'

'You tell Brigadier Aikens – personally – that he's facing a whole Komani clan, not just a few raiders, plus a large number of native rebels. They've got modern weapons of every type.'

'Yes sir.'

'All right – now get going.'

'But – they're shootin' to kill. You can't . . .'

'Sergeant, are you a soldier or a lawyer?'

Vorgens could sense McIntyre's face going red. 'Yes sir.'

'Now get moving. Don't worry about me. I've got something else in mind. Good luck to you both.'

'Luck to you, sir.'

They scrambled off down the gulley. Vorgens waited a moment, then headed across the gulley and up the other side. Once there, he started diagonally away from the spot where he had left McIntyre and Giradaux, toward the on-coming Komani.

As he scuttled through the foliage, he spotted three Komani warriors groping cautiously through the twilight haze. *The effect of the mescal's worn off*, he realized as he stopped to watch them.

Vorgens edged carefully off to one side of the approaching Komani, working his way to a position as far as possible from the direction the Terrans had taken. Another flare burst overhead, and in its sudden light Vorgens saw another trio of warriors moving slowly through the brush toward him. *Now is the time*, he said to himself.

He fired at the first group of Komani, hit two of them and left the third to scream for aid. Then he swung around and fired quickly at the other trio. He dropped one of them and got a sizzling blast by his ear in return.

Ducking into the deeper brush as the flare petered out, Vorgens crawled farther away from the Komani searchers, always leading them – he hoped – away from the escaping Terrans.

Twice more flares bloomed overhead, and twice Vorgens stopped to hit-and-run, making certain that the Komani knew from which direction he was firing.

Then for a long stretch there was dark silence. Vorgens squatted in the foliage and waited, straining his senses for some hint of what they were doing. He began to realize how a mouse might feel, if a pack of cats were quietly stalking it.

I wonder if they have infra-red snoopers? Then they wouldn't need flares. His answer was a sudden, searing flash, and a long, long fall into oblivion.

CHAPTER SIX

OKATAR

The darkness lifted slowly, and Vorgens gradually became aware that he was lying in a cot. There was no pain, no feeling whatsoever. He was aware that his eyes were open, but he was unable to focus them. The world was a gray blur. He tried to move, but found he could not. The effort was too great. He lapsed back into unconsciousness.

He awoke again. This time he could see. Things were still blurry, smeared at the edges, but he could see.

A girl was sitting by his cot, watching him, completely unaware that he was conscious and his eyes could function again. Her face was a curious mixture of anxiety and interest, as though she were looking into a mirror to find some flaw in herself. She was young and slim, with jet-black hair falling to her shoulders and wide, dark eyes.

Gradually, the girl's image became indistinct, and his head began throbbing painfully. Vorgens found himself slipping back into darkness again.

Then he heard voices. There were two of them, speaking a language he either did not understand or could not grasp through the ache in his head. Slowly his eyes focused on the glowing roof of the Komani bubble-tent. Vorgens found that he could turn his head slightly. He saw Sittas, deep in conversation with the Shinarian girl, who was standing now near the entrance to the tent. They were speaking something close to the Shinarian language he had been taught, Vorgens finally realized, probably an up-country dialect.

Vorgens closed his eyes, momentarily, he thought, but when he opened them again, the girl was gone and Sittas was standing alone by his cot.

'What time is it?' the Star Watchman asked.

The priest smiled. 'Past midday. You have been unconscious all night and morning.'

'What are you grinning at?'

'Your Terran training. Only a Terran would awake from

56

many hours of unconsciousness and ask what time of day it is.'

Vorgens propped himself up on an elbow. 'Time is getting to be important . . .'

'How do you feel?' the priest asked.

'Not bad. My head hurts a bit. How seriously was I hit?'

'You took a strong bolt from a sonic gun. I have no way of knowing how seriously the shock might have affected your nervous system.'

'There's one way to find out,' Vorgens said. He pushed himself up to a sitting position, and with Sittas' help got to his feet. 'A little wobbly,' he said, walking slowly across the tent with the old man at his elbow, 'but I think I'm all right.'

'You should try to eat,' the priest said, gesturing to a tray of food on the small table in the middle of the tent.

Vorgens nodded. 'How about the other two? Did they get away safely?'

'Yes,' Sittas answered. He hesitated for a moment, then said, 'Perhaps it is not proper for me to ask, but I do not understand how they escaped successfully and you did not.'

Vorgens sat down on a stool, next to the table.

'I didn't want to escape,' the Watchman said.

Sittas' mouth formed an unspoken *why?*

'It was necessary for someone to get back to the Mobile Force and warn Brigadier Aikens of the odds he's facing,' Vorgens explained. 'McIntyre can do that. Giradaux is better off with the sergeant than here. But I have a mission to carry out – a mission that calls for me to see Okatar Kang. You said he would not see an ordinary officer, only someone of high rank or great fighting ability.'

'That is true.'

'Please tell him, then,' Vorgens said, 'that the Star Watchman who engineered the escape of the two prisoners last night from under his nose has a message for him from the Commander-in-Chief of the Terran Imperial Star Watch.'

Sittas' weathered old face slowly unfolded into a broad grin. 'It might work.'

The priest left to try to reach Okatar and arrange a meeting. Vorgens sat alone at the tiny table and nibbled on some of the meat and fruit from the tray.

He smiled wryly at the irony of the situation: *Brigadier*

Aikens tries to prevent me from negotiating with the Komani, and his very orders bring me almost face-to-face with the Komani chieftain.

After a few minutes the Watchman got up and returned to his cot. The ache in his head was nearly gone, and the food had refreshed him. He stretched out on the cot, not to rest, but to think.

Vorgens tried to push every unwanted thought out of his mind, to reach back to his classes at the Academy, to remember what he had been taught about the Komani. He pictured in his mind the stereocast lecture he had sat through.

'A nation of warriors, consisting of nomadic clans that fight each other almost as often as they raid their neighbors. Their culture is feudal, their energies directed toward battle and loot. Komani warriors are disdainful of civilized values . . .'

Yet through it all Vorgens heard in the back of his mind the keening funeral dirge of the women; the solemn, frightened-yet-brave face of the youth who had brought them food the night before; the calm, firm insistence of Sittas that despite politics and wars, the Komani had souls.

How to appeal to them? That was the question. How to present the Star Watch's demands in a way that they could understand and accept? Vorgens thought about it, and tried to frame the words he would use with Okatar.

At length, Sittas returned to the tent. He stood silently at the entrance for several minutes before the Watchman noticed him there.

'Well?'

The old priest looked into Vorgens' eyes. 'You asked me to arrange a meeting with Okatar Kang.'

'That's right.'

'He wants to see you immediately.'

Vorgens jumped to his feet. 'Good!'

'No, my friend, not good,' Sittas murmured slowly. 'He wishes to see you merely to pronounce a death sentence over you.'

Vorgens was escorted to Okatar Kang's huge golden bubble-tent by a half-dozen warriors. Sittas walked at his side as they tramped through the encampment. The sun was high, the skies cloudless. The Watchman could not help but notice that there was much more bustle and activity in the Komani camp than there had been the previous afternoon.

They're pulling in their men from all over the planet, Vorgens said to himself. *They're getting ready for a major attack on the Mobile Force.*

He had expected the Kang's tent to be crowded with people, but instead it was nearly empty. A small group of Komani and Shinarians were sitting at a low-slung table off to one side of the tent. The guards marched Vorgens to the middle of the tent, then turned to face the table. Sittas remained just inside the doorway.

Vorgens guessed that the second Komani from the right was Okatar. He was no bigger or more impressive physically than the rest, but his head was held a trifle higher, his back was a shade stiffer, and his yellow cat's eyes gave an impression of unquestioned authority. Komani faces gave Vorgens a feeling of fierceness. He almost expected them to have saber-like fangs jutting from their lips.

Vorgens recognized Merdon among the Shinarians. The young rebel was going over a long list with Okatar while the others at the table listened in silence. For several minutes, Vorgens and his six guards stood in the middle of the tent, while Okatar carefully ignored them.

Finally he put the list down on the table and turned to face Vorgens.

'I am Okatar Kang,' he said, in standard Terran, 'and you are the Terran prisoner who tried to escape last night. Prisoners who spurn our hospitality are traditionally executed. Therefore . . .'

'Before you go any farther . . .' Vorgens began.

'Silence!' roared one of the Komani nobles.

Okatar glanced at the roarer, then returned to Vorgens. 'Pleas for mercy will not avail you.'

'I am not pleading for mercy,' Vorgens said, 'and I did not try to escape from your camp last night. If I had wanted to escape, I could have done so easily with my two fellow prisoners.'

'You aided their escape,' said another Komani noble, 'so the death penalty still holds.'

Sittas interrupted. 'He is not a true Terran,' the old priest said, walking up from the doorway toward the table, 'and has never been in contact with the Komani before. Your customs and laws are probably strange to him . . .'

Vorgens disagreed. 'I am familiar with your customs. I helped the two Terrans escape because I knew they would be put to death ultimately by you. Which of you would have done less for his own men?'

Okatar gave a grunt of grudging approval. 'And why did you not escape with them?'

'Because I have come to this planet to see you, Okatar. I have been sent by the Star Watch to offer you peace.'

'You were taken prisoner in a skirmish that cost us a score of lives,' one of the Komani countered. 'You were fighting from within an armored cruiser. What kind of peace offer is that?'

'My mission to this planet is to discuss a truce with you,' Vorgens insisted, talking straight to the Kang. 'Last night, we could have killed many more of your men. Instead we merely stunned them. I am not here to kill, but to save lives.'

Okatar glanced at Merdon, then, smiling grimly, said, 'I have heard of the peace offer you made to the Shinarian fighters. Do you presume to offer the same terms to the clan of Okatar?'

'If you leave Shinar at once and return to your home-world without further bloodshed,' Vorgens said, 'the Star Watch will take no punitive action against you.'

'And if we do not leave Shinar immediately?'

'You will be destroyed by the forces of the Terran Empire.'

Dead silence filled the room for a moment. Vorgens added, 'The Empire has half a galaxy of resources to pit against you . . . powerful armies and fleets. You cannot hope to overcome them all.'

'No, not by ourselves,' Okatar said quietly.

'I have also been instructed to inform you that the other Komani clan chiefs have sworn to the Empire that they will remain loyal and will not assist you, regardless of what you do.'

The slightest trace of a smile flickered across Okatar's grim face.

'I see,' he replied. 'Our choice is to return meekly home, or suffer complete destruction. Now then, about this destruction, where are the Imperial forces that will accomplish this mighty victory? Your Mobile Force is trapped and living on borrowed time. Your vaunted Star Watch fleets are nowhere near Shinar, and cannot get here within a month, at least.'

How does he know that? Vorgens wondered.

The Kang continued, 'Your mighty Empire has no military arm that can withstand the Komani peoples. One small clan of us has humbled your Mobile Force and planetary garrison. By this time tomorrow the word will be spreading through the galaxy that the Komani are on the march. Shinar is the beginning. The other clans will join us. In fact,' Okatar leaned forward and lowered his voice, conspiratorially, 'how can you be sure that *all* the warriors on Shinar are really members of my clan?'

Vorgens felt as though he had been shot again. Slowly, he answered, 'What you are saying is that you propose to cause a galactic war between the Komani clans and the Terran Empire. You cannot win such a war. The Empire has resources that will crush you; it will only be a matter of time – and lives.'

Okatar waved down the Star Watchman. 'No, my naive Terran. Not at all. Your Empire is crumbling already. If you had the strength to crush us, you would do it now, here, on this planet. Instead you send a small Mobile Force that will be extinguished in another day.

'The people of Shinar do not want your Empire. The people of the galaxy have learned to hate the Terrans. How do you think the Terrans gained control of their Empire? By taking it from the Masters. Now the Komani will take it from the Terrans. For too long now the Komani have fought each other, while the Terrans gained strength from our weakness. But that time is drawing to a close. When the other Komani clans see that the Terrans can be humbled in battle, they will join the clan of Okatar. Your Empire is ripe for picking.'

'You are going to plunge the galaxy into hell all over again,' Vorgens said, 'and you will not live to see the end of the chaos you cause.'

'Perhaps,' the Kang retorted, 'but certainly you will not live to see even the beginning. Unfortunately, we do not have the time to enjoy the ceremonial execution that bearers of ultimatums are traditionally given. Therefore, you shall be shot, before the sun sets.'

With that, Okatar nodded to the guards. One of them seized Vorgens' arm and turned him around. They marched out of the tent.

Vorgens walked blindly, numbly, seeing nothing and hearing nothing, his mind in a dizzying whirl that pulled in tighter and tighter on itself.

The Komani aren't interested in a peaceful settlement. They want only war. Aikens was right. He was right! This battle, here on this minor planet, is only the opening skirmish in a war that will engulf the whole galaxy. The Empire is in danger. Humankind is in danger. If the Empire crumbles, nine people out of every ten will starve. If the Komani have their way, the whole fabric of civilization will be destroyed.

They want to destroy, to kill. They want to kill me. I will be executed. Shot. Killed. Dead.

CHAPTER SEVEN

ALTAI

Merdon sat at the low-slung table, feeling slightly uncomfortable in the overlarge Komani chair, and watched Vorgens walk numbly out of the tent, escorted by the six guards. Sittas remained at the doorway for a moment, and Merdon's eyes met the old priest's and held there. Sittas' face was expressionless, but Merdon knew what was in his mind.

The Shinarian youth turned away and glanced at Romal and his other lieutenants, sitting at the table with him. When he looked back at the doorway, Sittas had gone.

'To return to these tallies of weapons . . .' Okatar said.

Merdon focused his attention on the Kang. 'One moment, I have never heard you talk before about this plan for conquering the entire Terran Empire. I would like to hear exactly how you propose to do it, and how your plans affect Shinar.'

Okatar smiled. 'In a few days – a few weeks, at most – the Komani will have left Shinar. The Terrans will be wiped out, and before they can bring more troops to your planet, we will have struck somewhere else, closer to the heart of their Empire. When we leave you, Shinar will be free of the Terrans for all time, never fear.'

Merdon said, 'But you are using Shinar as a stepping-stone in your plans against the Empire.'

'Of course. What of it? We will free Shinar of the Terrans. Our motives are inconsequential.'

'But do you really believe that you can defeat the Empire? With all their resources and manpower, the Terrans . . .'

Okatar's smile vanished. 'The resources and manpower of the Terrans come from worlds like your own. They are stolen from peoples who will gladly rise up against the Terrans, as they rose against the Masters a century ago. All they need is a leader, and an army to join. The Komani will be that army, and I will be that leader.'

'After you've defeated the Empire, what then? Will the Komani become the new masters of the galaxy?'

'In a sense, yes. But we will not become like the Terrans. We are fighters, not governors. The Komani will live on tribute, freely given by the peoples we liberate from the Terrans. We shall leave all peoples in peace, and fight against only those who work for the Terrans, or who oppose us.'

Merdon nodded. 'I see.' But in his mind he saw his father's worried face, and heard his words of warning.

'Now then,' Okatar resumed, 'about these tallies of weapons. I had assumed that there would be more weapons available. This list seems too short.'

Merdon could sense Romal, sitting next to him, tense at the Komani's question. He answered calmly:

'My quartermaster has prepared very accurate tallies. Remember that we took those weapons from small garrison posts among the outlying towns. The Terrans kept most of their weapons in the major arsenals in the four cities that they still hold.'

Okatar nodded. 'I understand that there are good-sized arsenals in some of the smaller cities. The port of Katan, for instance.'

'There is an arsenal there, yes,' Merdon agreed. 'But it is relatively small and nearly empty. Besides, Katan is a long distance from here. We could never get the weapons from the arsenal to our troops in time for tomorrow morning's attack on the Mobile Force.'

'Sound logic,' Okatar said. 'In any event, we have more than enough weapons for tomorrow's attack.' His lips parted in a smile, but his yellow eyes were cold.

'I have the latest information about food deliveries,' Romal said, changing the subject. His voice, always high-pitched, nearly cracked from nervousness.

They discussed the questions of provisions and other logistics problems for another hour. Neither Okatar nor Merdon mentioned the weapons again, or the arsenal in Katan. But both knew that the other was thinking hard about the matter.

When Merdon finally left Okatar's tent, he started back

toward his own quarters, with his four top lieutenants accompanying him. As they made their way through the Komani bubble-tents, Altai came up and joined them.

'My uncle would like to speak with you,' she said, striding along beside Merdon.

'It will have to wait. There are other things to do.'

She looked up at him. 'I heard that Okatar made a speech.'

Merdon grinned humorlessly. 'Several of them. He announced his plans for crushing the Empire, told us that he will expect us to support him by paying his clan tribute, and showed quite a bit of suspicion about the weapons tallies.'

'He knows that we're keeping back some weapons?'

'He suspects.'

'What are you going to do?' Altai asked.

'I'm going to hold a conference with my four best men, and we'll decide on what to do.'

'A conference? In your tent?'

'No,' Merdon said, shaking his head. 'Right out here, in the open. We're going to stroll around the camp and talk. I don't want to go to the tent . . . too much of a chance that a microphone might be hidden there.'

Altai nodded in agreement. 'All right. I'll wait for you at your tent.'

'No. Stay with us. We might look a little less as though we're plotting something if there's a girl with us.'

'A girl?' Altai repeated. 'Just any old girl? Just someone to make the Komani think you couldn't possibly be talking about anything serious?'

'Now don't be silly,' Merdon said, taking her hand in his. 'Of all the girls on the planet of Shinar, there is none that I would rather have standing here beside me, dazzling the Komani with her radiant beauty, more than you. There, are you happy now?'

Altai shrugged noncommittally. 'May I join the discussion, or must I merely listen?'

Merdon glanced at the other four. They were grinning broadly.

'You may speak,' he said, 'if you have something serious to say. This is a serious matter.'

'Yes I know,' Altai countered. 'But it's good to see you all smiling again. You looked so solemn a minute ago.'

'For good reason,' Merdon said.

'Okatar Kang thinks that the Komani can conquer the whole Terran Empire. Shinar is just the first step in his plan,' Romal said, his voice squeaking in excitement.

'We face the prospect,' Merdon said calmly, 'of having the Komani as overlords after the Terrans have been driven away.'

Altai shuddered involuntarily. 'They wouldn't even try to govern us. They would take whatever they wanted by force.'

The others murmured agreement.

'Don't be so sure,' Merdon argued. 'If the Komani are going to tackle the whole Terran Empire, they won't want to be bothered by uprisings in their rear. If they act belligerently toward us, we can fight. Okatar knows that.'

'Yes, and he knows his warriors can whip us,' said Tarat, the lanky son of a farmer, who now served as Merdon's chief tactician. 'Our men are willing fighters, but – I hate to admit it – we're just not strong enough or experienced enough to stop the Komani.'

'The Komani could whip us,' Merdon agreed. 'But not if they were fighting the Terrans at the same time.'

'You're walking out on a slender branch,' Tarat said.

'Without a safety field to catch you if you slip,' Altai added.

Merdon stopped walking and looked at them. They had reached the edge of the encampment, and were near a clump of tall trees. Beyond the grove shimmered the barely visible energy screen that protected the camp from missiles and force beams.

'Let's consider the basic things first,' Merdon said. 'Are we agreed that we want to be rid of the Terrans?'

'Not if it means living under the Komani,' Romal said stubbornly.

'Of course not,' Merdon said. 'But if we can be free, should we fight for freedom, or remain under the Empire?'

'Freedom!' snapped Tarat. 'Freedom or death. We've come too far to turn back now.'

'Right,' Merdon agreed. 'Even if we wanted to return to the Empire, the Terrans would never trust us again. We would all end up in exile, or worse.'

66

'No,' Altai said. 'Uncle Sittas said that the Terran Watchman . . .'

Merdon's scowl silenced her. 'The Watchman brought us an ultimatum – stop fighting or be wiped out by the Imperial troops. He never said what would happen after we stopped fighting. You can guess at what the Terrans would do.'

Altai stared at the rebel leader, her face set in a perplexed frown.

Merdon went on, as they resumed walking, 'At the moment, the Komani have the same aim that we do – to drive the Terrans off Shinar. Good. We can work together toward that goal.'

'And afterward?' Romal piped.

'Afterward, the Komani will want to attack another planet of the Empire. Again good. We will help them. We will provide them with all the food we can gather. We will give them ships, and clothing, and any equipment we have.'

'Weapons?'

'We will give them weapons, too. Half of all the weapons taken from the arsenals at the four major cities. The other half we will keep. All the other weapons we are now holding on to – including the arsenal in Katan – we shall keep.'

'And if Okatar finds out?' Altai asked softly.

'It will be no secret. We will tell him that we are keeping these weapons in case we are attacked. We have a right to defend ourselves, if we are free.'

Tarat grunted in sudden understanding. 'Woof. You'll be telling Okatar that if he tries to take anything else from Shinar, we'll fight him.'

'That's right,' Merdon said. 'We'll be perfectly willing to have him fight the Terrans elsewhere, and leave Shinar in peace.'

'You're gambling,' Tarat said, 'that Okatar will prefer to fight the Terrans rather than us.'

'He'll have more to gain fighting the Empire. There's no profit – and no glory for him – in staying here and crushing us.'

The four lieutenants muttered among themselves.

'I know this is a hard decision to make,' Merdon said. 'We're running a terrible risk. If things don't work out well, we'll see our world turned into a blood-soaked shambles. We

67

will be killed, no doubt. But if we're smart enough, and strong enough . . . we can achieve freedom. Is it worth the risk or not?'

'It is!' Tarat said.

Romal nodded unhappily. 'I guess there's no other way.'

The others agreed.

Altai remained silent. But Merdon could read the question in her eyes: *Is there no other way? Is there absolutely no other possible way?*

In a small chamber within his main tent, Okatar Kang watched the six young Shinarian rebels on a tabletop viewscreen as they walked back from the trees at the edge of the camp and returned to their own tents.

'The remote receptor picks up their every word, does it not, my lord?' asked the Komani noble at his elbow.

'Indeed so,' Okatar said. 'My compliments to the technicians.'

'You have seen enough?'

Okatar nodded. 'Yes. Quite enough.'

The four lieutenants scattered to their private tents, while Altai accompanied Merdon back to his own quarters. Inside the plastic bubble, Sittas was sitting quietly, his eyes closed. The old priest looked up as the two youngsters entered.

'Were you sleeping or praying?' Merdon asked jokingly.

'A little of both, I fear.'

Merdon sat on a corner of the table and faced the priest. Altai stood beside her uncle's chair.

'You want to talk to me about the Watchman.'

Sittas nodded. 'You must ask Okatar to pardon him. Keep him a prisoner if you must, but a cold-blooded execution . . .'

Merdon held up three fingers. 'First, Okatar would not pardon a man he has sentenced to death. The Komani aren't interested in clemency. Secondly, the Watchman has killed Komani warriors, and can hardly be treated as an innocent ambassador of good-will. Thirdly, if he got back to the Terrans he would end up by killing our own people. So how can you ask for mercy?'

'This Watchman is not an ordinary Terran,' Sittas began.

'I know,' Merdon interrupted. 'He's worse. He knows the
68

Terrans conquered his nation, and yet he fights for the Terrans. He's an enemy – by his own choice and his own admission.'

'A very unusual enemy,' Sittas countered. 'On the whole planet of Shinar, this youth is the only one who has mentioned the word peace in seriousness since the rebellion began. I believe that he holds the key to peace on Shinar.'

'Peace under the Empire? Never. That would merely be returning to the situation that caused the rebellion in the first place.'

'It doesn't have to be that way, Merdon,' Altai said.

'It doesn't? Why not? Because we don't want things to be that way? Because we dream of a world ruled by our own people, without the Terrans or anyone else standing on our necks? Well how is this wonderful world going to come about? By prayer? By dreaming? By longing for peace, at any price?'

Merdon pounded a fist onto his open palm. 'We must fight for freedom! The Terrans will not give us freedom for the asking. The Komani will not leave us alone unless we are strong enough to discourage them from attacking us. Is peace worth slavery? Is life so precious that we would place our worthless hides above freedom for our people, above freedom for the generations that haven't even been born? No. We will fight, and keep fighting, until we have our freedom. Then peace will come, and we will welcome it as men, not as spineless dogs.'

Sittas smiled and nodded. 'Fine oratory. It will sound stirring in the history books, but I am not convinced that unending warfare will bring peace to Shinar – or freedom. This Star Watchman, Vorgens, might possibly turn the trick for you. In the vast Terran Empire, there must be officials who would be willing to listen to our cause, and work out some solution satisfactory to all of us.'

'No such Terran has ever taken an interest in Shinar. I doubt that such a Terran exists.'

'Perhaps the Watchman could help us to find the right officials.'

'The Watchman is a prisoner and sentenced to die,' Merdon repeated doggedly. 'Your dreams of finding peace are nothing but wishful thinking. The Watchman is only a junior officer. Do you think he could actually command a truce here on Shinar? Do you think the commander of the Imperial Marines takes orders from a junior officer? The Watchman has no power, no authority. His life is worthless.'

The old priest slowly rose, trembling, from his chair. 'The strain of your duties has taken its toll on your good sense, Merdon, and on your heart. Never in my life would I have expected you to say what you did a moment ago. A human life – worthless? You had better examine your conscience, my son. You are beginning to enjoy this war too much.'

Merdon started to reply, thought better of it, and simply sat there on the edge of the table, his eyes meeting the priest's. Finally Sittas turned and silently walked out of the tent.

'The old fool,' Merdon grumbled. 'He knows I didn't mean it that way.'

Altai asked, 'How did you mean it?'

'Now don't you start arguing against me!'

She looked at Merdon's strong, stubborn face for a moment, then turned her eyes away and said, 'Merdon – many people have died since this fight began. My own village has been nearly wiped out, first by the Terrans and then by the Komani.'

'That raid was a misunderstanding.'

'Yes, I know. But many people were killed anyway. Dozens of our classmates were killed in the fighting at the university . . .'

'I remember. And you fought by my side during those early days.'

'Early days,' Altai mused. 'A few weeks ago. It seems like a lifetime has passed since then.'

'A lifetime has passed,' Merdon said. 'None of us is the same person he was before this began. We can never go back to those days, Altai. Never.'

'Merdon, listen to me. Please. Don't let this Watchman be killed. I don't know why, but I can't just stand back and allow a man to be executed. This war has already killed many, many good people. But they were killed in battle. Now – now you're going to let them come in and shoot him. You can't let it happen!'

The young rebel shook his head. 'Altai, it has to be this

70

way. There's no other way. He's a Komani prisoner, not ours. We can't set him free. We can't help him escape.'

'You mean you won't try to help him.'

'I can't.'

She drew herself up to her full height. Merdon smiled inwardly at her, trying to be as tall as a man.

'You can't help him,' Altai said, 'but there are others who can.'

Instantly, Merdon's amusement vanished. 'What do you mean by that?'

She started for the doorway. 'You'll see.'

'Altai! Don't do anything foolish. The Komani wouldn't hesitate to shoot a girl – or a priest.'

CHAPTER EIGHT

THROUGH THE FLAMES

Vorgens sat in stunned silence in the tent to which the guards had brought him. The Komani warriors loitered outside while the young Star Watchman stared at the blank wall of the tent.

The touch of a hand on his shoulder startled him. He looked up and saw Sittas standing beside him.

'Have courage,' the priest said quietly.

'Does it show? The fear?'

'Not much.'

Vorgens ran a hand through his close-cropped hair. 'You heard what Okatar said. The other Komani clans are in league with him. This is the beginning of a galaxy-wide war.'

Sittas shook his head. 'Not necessarily. The other clans may be giving him some aid, and no doubt they are giving him considerable encouragement, but they will not move in force until it becomes clear that the Empire is too weak to stop them.'

'If the Mobile Force is wiped out, that would be their signal, wouldn't it?'

'It could be.'

'They'll attack tomorrow morning, for certain,' Vorgens said. 'They've got more men and equipment than Aikens dreams they have. If he stands and fights in that valley, we'll lose Shinar and the whole Komani nation will begin to march against the Empire.'

But Sittas was no longer listening. He was standing at the doorway of the tent, looking out. The late afternoon sun slanting through the doorway touched his wispy hair and gave him a modest halo.

Vorgens stood up. 'Well, when is the firing squad coming? Or do they like to let their victims dangle for a few hours?'

'Death comes to us all, my friend,' Sittas murmured, still gazing intently outward.

'It's odd,' Vorgens said, pacing across the tent floor, 'I

never thought about how I would die. I've been aboard starships that have run into trouble – real trouble. And yesterday, in battle, and last night, helping McIntyre and Giradaux to escape, I was frightened, all right, but the thought of death – my death – it just never entered my mind. But now . . . I never thought I would die before a firing squad – on a planet I didn't even know existed until a few weeks ago.'

'If we knew the time and place of the end of our lives,' Sittas said, glancing at the Watchman, 'we would hardly find life interesting enough to go through with it.'

'That's not much help.'

The old priest smiled. 'Then perhaps your next visitor will have better words for you.'

Puzzled, Vorgens stepped over to the entrance of the tent, where Sittas was still standing. Walking through the Komani encampment toward them was a Shinarian girl. Vorgens recognized her as the girl he had seen while he was still half-unconscious after being shot.

'So she's not a dream,' he muttered.

'Altai? She is my niece. We are from the same village. She joined the rebel forces at the university where she met Merdon.'

Vorgens frowned. 'One of Merdon's rebels. So she hates the Terrans, too. And me. Just as Okatar said they all do.'

'She is too young to hate,' Sittas said.

They stepped back from the entryway as Altai walked into the tent. The girl looked at Vorgens for a moment, then turned to her uncle and nodded silently.

Sittas said, to no one in particular, 'Let us pray for guidance.'

The old man stood a few paces from the entrance, and began chanting. But his eyes were on Vorgens, and he gestured with one hand, first pointing to his ear, then to the guards outside.

Vorgens smiled in understanding. Altai pulled a low bench up to the table in the middle of the room and sat down. Vorgens sat next to her. She took a thin slip of plasti-film and a stylus from the waistband of her slacks and began drawing as Vorgens watched.

Altai sketched the tent they were in, and a dozen nearby tents. In two of the circles she drew she wrote a single word:

ammunition. Then she put down a pair of wavy lines, running parallel from Vorgens' tent outward to the edge of the film. Within the lines she wrote *safe lane*; outside the lines, on both sides, she wrote *fire*.

She looked up at Vorgens to see if he understood. Vorgens nodded, and noticed that her eyes were as black and deep as space itself.

While Sittas continued to chant, Altai gestured toward the wall of the tent. Then she touched the stylus on the word *fire*.

Vorgens shook his head and whispered, 'Nonflammable. Will not burn.'

Altai smiled and whispered back, 'Thermal grenade. It will burn.'

Vorgens grinned at her. 'How soon?'

'As quickly as possible,' she answered, rolling up the film and tucking it back into her waistband.

They stood up together. Altai was nearly Vorgens' own height. Sittas finished his chant.

'I hope our prayers are answered,' the priest said.

Vorgens watched the two of them leave the tent. He stood at the entrance as the old man and the girl walked slowly away and finally disappeared behind some of the gaudy Komani bubble-tents.

The Watchman stepped back toward the middle of the tent. *Now it's a race to see who is ready first: Sittas and his niece, or Okatar's execution detail.*

His answer – several minutes later – was a dull booming sound and the jarring smack of a concussion wave that jolted everything in the tent. Another explosion, ear-splitting, knocked Vorgens off his feet and toppled the table next to him. A Komani warrior stuck his head through the entrance as Vorgens was climbing to his feet. Shouts and screams were mixing with a series of explosions and the peculiar *whoosh* sound of huge sheets of flame leaping skyward. Vorgens could hear men running outside, and saw behind his guard's back the eerie, flickering light that could only be coming from a huge blaze.

The warrior ducked through the entryway and motioned to Vorgens with a huge, pawlike hand.

'Out. Danger. Fire.'

Vorgens stalled. 'You mean you're worried about me?'

74

The Komani took another step toward Vorgens, and fingered the pistol on his hip.

The whole far end of the tent suddenly dissolved into flames. The Komani gave an involuntary shriek and leaped for the entrance. Vorgens, without time to think about it, dived straight into the burning plastic wall.

He jumped headfirst, as hard and as far as his legs could catapult him. He landed, hands down on cool moist grass, and somersaulted. Getting to his feet, Vorgens saw that Altai's plan was working just as her sketch had shown.

The dome of the tent behind him was engulfed in fire. Flaming tents stretched off on either side of him, but the ground between them was clear. The heat was intense though. Not even the grass would last long at this rate.

Vorgens took off at top speed, straight down the alley of fire, legs pumping as hard as they could, lungs sucking in searing, spark-filled air. Smoke burned at his eyes and he could feel that parts of his face and hands were scorched.

Finally he was free of the flames and stumbling down the shrub-choked slope that marked the edge of the meadow and the end of the Komani camp. Gasping for breath, exhausted and riddled with pain, he sprawled in the bushes.

For several minutes he lay there, chest heaving, legs aching, watching the heavy black smoke, occasionally mixed with tongues of flame, billowing from the Komani camp.

'Are you all right?'

Startled, he turned to see Altai kneeling beside him.

'Yes. I'll be fine as soon as I catch my breath.'

'The Komani will have the fire out soon,' she said. 'We'd better move quickly.'

Vorgens scrambled to his feet. 'I'm ready.'

Silently she led him deeper into the brush, past a clump of tall trees. Beyond the trees stood Sittas, his robes tinged red by the last rays of the sinking sun.

'I took the liberty', Altai said as they approached the priest, 'of borrowing three flyers from one of the Komani tents that I had to set on fire. They will never miss them.'

'*You* set on fire? You mean you did all that . . . yourself?'

She nodded and tried not to look smug, but Vorgens could see that she was proud of herself. 'It wasn't too difficult. None of the tents was occupied. The Komani used them

75

for storing ammunition and equipment. All it took was a couple of small grenades to set off everything.'

'And a lot of courage,' Vorgens added.

By this time they were close enough for Sittas to join the conversation. 'You made it safely,' the old priest said.

'A few singes here and there, but I'm still alive.'

'It'll be dark soon,' Altai said. 'We'd better wait for a while before trying to take off on the flyers.'

They spent the last few minutes of daylight examining the saddle-like, one-man Komani flyers. None of them had ridden one before, but after a few tests of the controls, Vorgens showed them how to handle it.

Night finally came, softened by the ever-present airglow. A flicker of fire still rose from the Komani camp.

Vorgens straddled his flyer and touched the buttons on the pummel that activated the machine. The flyer seemed to pulse into life. It stirred and vibrated, as though waiting for a command to action. He glanced at Sittas and Altai. They both seemed ready to go, although Vorgens worried about the priest's ability to handle the machine.

At a nod from Altai they started off, keeping low and sticking as much as possible to the shadows until they were well away from the Komani camp. Then they soared above tree-top level and made better time.

As they skimmed along, Vorgens allowed Sittas to set the pace for them. The old man had some difficulty managing the flyer, but with Vorgens and Altai staying side by side with him, they got along without any real trouble.

They flew toward the valley where the Mobile Force was encamped, and landed on a hillside nearby, after less than an hour's flight. They edged the flyers into the bushes, where they would be reasonably safe from discovery.

'I'll go the rest of the way on foot,' Vorgens said. 'If I tried flying over the guard posts at night they'd shoot me down automatically.'

Sittas nodded. 'What will you do after you get there?'

'I've got to convince Brigadier Aikens to break out of this valley. He's hopelessly outnumbered if he sits there and tries to battle it out. There'll be a slaughter . . . on both sides.'

'If you do get the Terran forces out of this trap, what then?'

76

Vorgens shook his head. 'I don't know. We'll be buying time. We'll be saving lives. That's enough for now.'

'Okatar plans to attack at dawn,' Altai said, 'from the side of the valley that will give him the sun at his back.'

'I expected that,' Vorgens said. 'Where will Merdon's forces be? I'd rather avoid firing on Shinarians, if it can be helped.'

In the semi-darkness, Vorgens could not see Altai's eyes widen in surprise and joy. There was a moment's hesitation before she answered.

'Our people will be directly on Okatar's left flank, and one thing more, the Komani are pulling back most of their men from this end of the valley, so that they can mount a stronger attack at sunrise. There will be only a thin screen of warriors in this area.'

'Then we could break through,' Vorgens said, 'if we hit them with everything we have.'

'Yes,' Altai agreed, 'and without firing on Shinarians.'

'You must tell your commander,' Sittas reminded, 'that a defeat here may well touch off a galactic war.'

'I know. I know.'

Sittas looked up at the sky. 'You have only until dawn. You must move quickly.'

'I . . . there are no words to thank you enough,' Vorgens said, 'not just for your help – but for my life.'

The priest smiled and put a hand on his shoulder. 'Go quickly. And good fortune to you.'

'What about you and Altai?'

'We will be safe enough. This is our homeworld, remember.'

Vorgens nodded. He turned to Altai. 'Thank you, too. I hope that the fighting is ended quickly.'

He wanted to say more, then decided against it. He turned away from them and started down the grassy slope of the hill toward the Mobile Force.

Okatar Kang stood watching the smoldering ruins of the tents, with several of his nobles beside him. His face was an impassive mask as Komani warriors sprayed and beat out the last glowing embers.

77

Merdon walked up slowly, alone except for a single Komani escort.

'It was a stubborn fire,' Merdon said.

Okatar looked down at the young rebel. Though tall for a Shinarian, Merdon barely stood as high as the Komani Kang's shoulder.

'Several cases of Terran thermal grenades made the fire difficult to fight,' Okatar said.

'This was an unfortunate time for such an accident,' Merdon said. 'With the attack . . .'

Okatar cut him short. 'This fire will have no effect on our attack. And it was no accident. It was deliberate sabotage.'

'Deliberate? You can't mean it.'

Okatar said nothing.

'But who would do such a thing?' Merdon asked.

'I was hoping you might be able to tell me. Obviously no Komani would destroy his own tents and some of his precious ammunition.'

Merdon nodded and remained silent for a few moments, his mind racing. Then he asked, 'Wasn't the Watchman quartered near here?'

'Yes,' Okatar said, gesturing toward a patch of charred earth. 'That was where his tent stood.'

'Where is he now?'

Okatar shrugged. 'We have found no sign of him.'

'Then it must have been him! He knew he was going to be executed, so he somehow set this fire, trying to cause damage to us. He probably died in his own flames.'

Okatar's yellow eyes flickered with amusement. 'An engaging theory. However, there are three flaws in it. First, we have not found his remains among the ruins.'

'His body could have been totally consumed . . .'

'Second,' Okatar continued, ignoring Merdon, 'one of my warriors saw the Watchman inside his own tent *after* the first explosions. The fire had already started.'

'Could he have—'

'And finally,' Okatar went on, relentlessly, 'we have the very curious pattern of the fire itself.'

Okatar pointed to one of the warriors standing nearby, and the Komani switched on a huge floodlight that bathed the whole area in brightness.

78

'Look carefully at the scene of the fire,' Okatar said to Merdon. 'Tell me what you see.'

Merdon said, 'Blackened ground where the flames were burning. Some withered grass nearby. What else?'

'Starting here, where the Watchman's tent stood,' Okatar said, striding to the scorched oval, 'and looking outward toward the edge of the camp – what do you see?'

Merdon looked out along the direction indicated by the Kang's outstretched arm. The evidence was clear: two lanes of fire-blacked ground, and between them, a path of safety that led to the edge of the camp.

'I see,' Merdon said at last.

'Yes,' Okatar answered. 'Now I ask you – who would have done this? Who would have committed this sabotage, and rescued the Watchman? One of my men, or one of yours?'

Merdon looked directly into the Komani chieftain's eyes. 'Perhaps neither,' he said evenly. 'Perhaps it was the two Terrans who had escaped. They might have returned to free their fellow-prisoner.'

'How would they know where he was being held?'

Merdon stroked his jaw for a moment. 'They could have been watching the camp from those trees. Or the Watchman might have had some sort of miniature signaling device hidden on him.'

Okatar nodded. 'Perhaps so. I had not considered that possibility.'

'My people have been fighting shoulder to shoulder with your warriors,' Merdon added. 'There is no reason to think that they would have aided the Watchman, and done this damage to our cause.'

'Perhaps,' Okatar muttered. 'Perhaps.'

'Still,' Merdon said, 'I will check with my people to see if they can shed any light on this.'

'Good.'

'The attack is still set for dawn?'

Okatar nodded.

'All right. I'd better get down there with my men.'

Merdon turned away and left the scene of the fire. Okatar gestured to the warrior at the light, and the Komani turned it off.

'Do you believe him?' asked one of the nobles.

'Of course not,' Okatar replied. 'There were six Shinarians present when I sentenced the Watchman to death: Merdon, his four underlings, and that priest. Send a man to check on each of them. If any one of them is missing, your man is to find him – no matter where on Shinar he may be, and when he finds him – kill him.'

'It shall be done.'

CHAPTER NINE

THE HOURS BEFORE DAWN

Brigadier Aikens sat in frowning silence for a moment as the Star Watchman stood before him. Vorgens looked bedraggled and utterly worn. His uniform was torn and grimy. There was an angry red burn on his right cheek.

Finally the brigadier hunched over his desk and jabbed a finger at Vorgens. 'Do you seriously expect me to believe this story?'

'Sir, if my word is not—'

'I don't doubt your word, Watchman. It's your judgment.' Aikens grinned humorlessly. 'Befriended by a native priest. Rescued from a firing squad. Tipped off to the Komani strategy and shown a route by which we can escape. Use your head, boy! You've been hoodwinked.'

'I can't believe that, sir,' Vorgens said quietly. 'I know what I saw.'

Aikens ran a hand over his balding dome. 'All right, what did you see? That the barbarians have more men and equipment than we thought? That some of the natives are on their side? That we can't count on reinforcements from the city garrisons? So what? It makes no difference on the military situation here.'

'But that's the whole point, sir,' Vorgens insisted, his voice still soft. 'The tactical situation here is overshadowed by the strategic importance of your decision. If the defeat of the Mobile Force is to be the signal for a general uprising of the Komani clans, then *strategically* you must withdraw and decline combat. You can't afford running the risk of a defeat at this time and place.'

'Are you lecturing me on military concepts?' Aikens got up slowly from his chair and his voice rose in pitch. 'My men can whip any horde of undisciplined barbarians, I don't care what their numbers are!'

'But the Komani are not undisciplined. They're as well trained as any troops in the galaxy. And the odds are overwhelmingly against you. If you fight here you will be wiped out. Your defeat will touch off a war of terrible proportions.'

Aikens thundered, 'I've served this Empire for more years than you've known, and on more planets than I care to remember, and I've never heard such panicked, sickening, fear-ridden talk in my life. If you think for one minute that I'll be scared into a withdrawal that'll be, at best, a humiliation to our uniforms, and might possibly lead to a well-planned ambush . . .'

'But, sir—'

'But nothing!' Aikens slammed a fist on his desk. 'Wake up, Watchman! Just because you're racially closer to these natives than to real Terrans doesn't mean that you have to swallow everything they tell you. They've fed you a fairy tale. There's nothing those savages would like better than to see my Force trying to sneak out of this valley. They'd cut us to ribbons between here and the next range of hills. That priest, and that girl you seem so entranced with – they're probably waiting for us up in those hills, with guns in their hands, waiting for us and laughing at you! It's a trap, Watchman. A trap set for a gullible young fool.'

Vorgens sucked in his breath. 'Sir, I cannot stand by and—'

'Just get out of my sight, mister, and stay out of my way.'

Aikens sat down again and turned his attention to the pile of reports on his desk.

'Brigadier Aikens, you don't realize what you're—'

'Dismissed.'

'But, sir—'

'*Dismissed!*'

Vorgens left the brigadier's office and walked blindly down the narrow passageway to the outer hatch. He climbed down to the ground and stood for a moment next to the mammoth dreadnaught, looking at the maze of vehicles spread across the valley floor, waiting for the dawn. Most of the men were sleeping, he knew – or trying to.

Can Aikens be right? Vorgens wondered. *What makes me so certain that I'm not wrong? He was right about Okatar Kang's reaction to the truce offer. It could be a trap. Sittas lying? Altai working for the Komani? Leading me and the whole Mobile Force into a slaughter? And yet . . . I went across those hills tonight. The Ko-*

mani really have pulled most of their men away. Can that be part of the trap? Whose judgment can I trust: my own, or Aikens'?

He began to walk away from the dreadnaught, looking for the cruiser in which he had been quartered. As he walked, he continued to question himself.

How long has Aikens been on Shinar?

A few weeks.

Has he met any of the native rebel leaders?

No.

Has he seen any of the Komani?

Only in battle.

What does he know about the situation on Shinar?

Only what he tells himself.

Then why was he right about Okatar's refusal of the truce?

Vorgens stopped for a moment and puzzled over that one. *He knew what Okatar would do,* the Watchman realized suddenly, *because that is exactly what Aikens himself would have done if he had been in Okatar's place.*

Aikens and Okatar! The same personality, really, when you strip away the differences in race and cultural background. Both warriors. Both impatient with anything less than battle. Both eager to fight it out, here in this valley.

Aikens doesn't want to retreat from the valley because he's anxious to meet Okatar in battle. His fear of a trap is just an excuse. Probably he doesn't realize it himself, but it's only an excuse. He *wants* to fight Okatar!

Vorgens frowned. *Or do I merely want to believe it, because I think Aikens is wrong?*

There was a way to verify his idea, Vorgens suddenly remembered. He turned back and half ran toward the dreadnaught. He clambered inside and made his way to the main computer. A dreadnaught's computer served an amazing variety of functions, from directing fire control to making statistical predictions of an enemy's intent. Vorgens was interested in the personnel records stored in the memory banks. The records were carried to allow officers to pick particularly qualified men for any given task. As a matter of course, the brigadier's battle history would be there.

The computer control center was a tiny compartment, consisting of a desk-console with its control keyboard, and a readout viewscreen. The cramped compartment was un-attended at this hour.

It took Vorgens a few minutes to figure out the coding system that unlocked the computer's memory banks, but finally he had Brigadier Aikens' battle record on the viewscreen.

Vorgens tensed in sudden shock as he read about Aikens' first major battle. It was in the Pleiades Uprising, the rebellion in which Vorgens' own grandfather had been killed.

So Aikens fought against my people, Vorgens said to himself.

The Star Watchman read the details of the record. Aikens was a junior officer then, and he did not see action on the planet where Vorgens' family lived.

Still, he doesn't think very highly of my people.

Vorgens read on. There were two other major battles in Aikens' record. His first action as a senior commander was a daring attack on the capital planet of the Saurian Federation. Vorgens recalled from his history courses that the Saurians had attempted to withdraw from the Terran Empire. Aikens' raid on their capital was the blow that collapsed them.

Vorgens scanned past scores of minor skirmishes, and then found the third major battle on the brigadier's record. It was against a Komani clan that was raiding a Terran planet. Aikens was in charge of the garrison. He had been awarded the Legion of Courage medal for his successful defense of the planet.

The citation that accompanied the medal read, in part, 'For heroically standing his ground in the face of overwhelming enemy superiority in numbers . . .'

So that's what he's up to, Vorgens thought. *He wants to repeat the tactics that won the medal.*

Vorgens flicked off the computer and leaned back in the chair before the control console. The record had made many things clear – Aikens' immediate dislike of Vorgens, and the brigadier's stubborn insistence on standing his ground and facing his enemies, no matter what their number and advantage.

Only one thing was not clear: what could Star Watch Junior Officer Vorgens do to correct the situation?

Impulsively, Vorgens tapped out another set of instructions on the computer keyboard. He spent a few more minutes reading very carefully the Star Watch regulations that appeared on the viewscreen in answer to his request.

Vorgens nodded to himself. He turned off the computer once again and stepped out of the tiny compartment into the passageway. At one end of the passageway was an open hatch, and Vorgens could see the sky beginning to pale.

The Watchman made his way to the dreadnaught's dispensary. A sleepy-eyed medic, gray-haired and sour-faced, was sitting next to the diagnostic booth, checking his inventory of supplies.

'I'll need some energy capsules that will keep me going at top efficiency for the next day.'

The medic looked up at him. 'When's the last time you slept?'

Vorgens had to think a moment. 'Night before last – until about noon.'

'Pills are no substitute for sleep.'

'Doctor, I have no time to argue.'

The medic got up from his chair and went to a cabinet. 'All right. But I want your name. I'll have to check on you. I don't want anybody living on pills.'

Vorgens grinned. 'Doctor, if we're both alive by the end of this day, you can check on me as much as you like.'

The medic handed him three orange capsules. 'That should keep you going for a whole day. Take one now, the others when you feel you need 'em.'

'Thank you. My name is Vorgens. Star Watch Junior Officer.'

Vorgens left the dreadnaught and trotted toward the cruiser where his quarters were. His thoughts were racing even faster than his body, though.

You know what you think and what you believe. Do you have the nerve to act on it? Do you have the strength to make a decision that will mean life or death for all the men in this valley? Can you shoulder that much responsibility?

He knew that, in reality, it did not matter whether he wanted to take the responsibility or not. It was his, and he could not escape it.

While Vorgens was arguing with Brigadier Aikens, Merdon was striding along the narrow crest of a ridge overlooking the valley where the Mobile Force lay huddled and waiting for the dawn.

The young Shinarian was inspecting his troops in the final hours before battle. In the softly lit night, he watched his rebels – students, farmers, young workers from the cities – as they cleaned their guns, checked their ammunition, went over their assignments with their squad leaders.

Tarat, walking beside Merdon, said, 'They're ready. They're primed and ready for the battle.'

Merdon nodded. As he stepped along the ridge, the young fighters – girls as well as men – recognized him and waved or grinned in greeting.

Beyond the crest of the ridge the ground sloped away toward the valley floor. The Terran forces there were hidden in shadow, but Merdon could sense their presence.

'Any activity tonight?' he asked Tarat, pointing a thumb toward the darkened valley floor.

The lanky tactician shook his head. 'They've been very quiet. A few patrols this morning, but they withdrew as soon as we offered some opposition. Since then, nothing.'

'H'm. Where are Romal and the others?'

'A little further down the line. They're waiting for you.'

'Good.'

'Say, have you told Altai to stay away from the battle?'

Merdon's head jerked upward involuntarily. 'Why . . . what makes you ask?'

'She hasn't been here all night. We thought she'd be coming with you, but she didn't. She's always been in the thick of everything – ever since the first fights at the university.'

'She'll be here,' Merdon said flatly.

'When? I mean, what's keeping her? She's our good luck charm.'

'She'll be here!'

Tarat stared at his chief for a moment, then decided to drop the subject. 'I've set up the command post up there,' he pointed, 'on that little knoll. Gives us a good view of the ridge and the whole valley.'

'Good.'

They climbed up the side of the knoll and stepped into

the dugout that had been cut into its crest. It had a bare, earthen floor and walls, and was roofless. Merdon glanced up at the sky. A few clouds were scudding across the stars.

'It's not going to rain, is it?'

Romal answered, 'We made a radio contact with our underground forces in Capital City. Their meteorologist predicts some cloudiness here for tomorrow, but no rain.'

Merdon turned from the little quartermaster to another of his lieutenants. 'Ron, you're a farmer. Will it rain tomorrow?'

Ron scratched his head. 'Shouldn't. But we might get a shower towards sundown.'

'So much for meteorology,' Merdon muttered.

He turned and surveyed the dugout. Portable communications equipment stood along one wall, with a table full of maps alongside it. Merdon went to the table and half sat against it.

'I assume everyone is ready for the attack, and you all know exactly what you're expected to do.'

They murmured agreement.

'I just want to call your attention to the basic job we've got to do. The Komani will be mounted on their flyers. They'll be the shock troops. Their mission is to hit the Terrans with beamguns and missiles, and knock out or neutralize the Terran armored vehicles.

'We'll be the infantry. We move in behind the Komani attack waves and mop up. We're the ones who'll actually board the Terran vehicles and smoke out their crews. It'll be tough, unspectacular, dangerous work. Our casualties will probably be high. But at the end of this day – before the showers that Ron predicts – the Terran Mobile Force will be wiped out. Within a week, the garrisons of the four cities either will have surrendered or been destroyed. Shinar will be free.'

None of the young leaders cheered, but Merdon could see the eagerness and determination in their eyes.

'Is this meeting for men only, or can a lowly female come in?' Altai asked, and without waiting for an answer she stepped into the command post. A beamgun was buckled at her hip, and a bandolier of grenades slung over one shoulder.

87

Merdon grinned at her. 'I was beginning to wonder what was keeping you.'

'You didn't think I'd stay away, did you?'

Their eyes met and locked for a long, wordless moment. Romal broke the silence. 'Did you see the fire in the Komani camp?' he squealed. 'It took them hours to get it out. Six tents full of stores and ammunition, up in smoke.'

'Yes,' Altai answered with a slight smile, 'I saw the fire.'

'And where is your uncle?' Merdon asked.

'He wanted to come, but I thought it would be better if he remained further back in the hills. The front line is no place for a man of his years.'

'True enough.'

'I'm not in the way, am I?' Altai asked. 'Did I interrupt?'

'No,' Tarat said, 'We were just leaving. There's nothing remaining to be done now except wait for the dawn's first light.'

'Good luck then,' Altai said to the four lieutenants as they filed out of the dugout.

When the last of them was out of earshot, Merdon took both her hands in his and said, 'I'm glad you came. I was worried about you.'

'We saw the Watchman back safely to the Terran forces.'

'It was a foolish thing for you to do. Foolish and futile.'

'Perhaps,' she answered. 'But I had to do it.'

'And yet you came back to fight against him.'

'Not against him, Merdon. For Shinar. No matter how much we differ about the Watchman, we are still together on the basic fact – Shinar will be free.'

While Merdon and Altai talked away the final hour before dawn, six Komani warriors huddled together in a trench not far from the Shinarian command post.

'Every one of the Shinarians is here except the old priest,' said one of the warriors.

Another of the warriors nodded. 'I cannot find him anywhere.'

'Then according to Lord Okatar's command,' said the first, 'he is the one responsible for the fire at camp.'

'Yes. I must find him, wherever he is hiding, and kill him.'

The six huge, cat-faced warriors agreed with solemn nods.

'I will miss the battle, then,' said the Komani.

'Better to miss the battle than to disobey the orders of your Kang.'

'True. Still, it is hard to turn one's back on a battle.'

'Lord Okatar will reward you greatly for your faithfulness.'

'If I find the priest.'

'There is no alternative. You may not return to our tents until you have carried out the Kang's command. The priest must die.'

'Yes.'

The warriors stood up and began to exchange farewells when, involuntarily, their ears pricked up.

'Listen?'

'What is it?'

A faint, far-off whining. A distant, high-pitched shrill.

'I know that sound,' said one of the Komani. 'It comes from Terran engines. They are starting up their cruisers and dreadnaughts. The battle is about to begin.'

CHAPTER TEN

TIME OF DECISION

Vorgens reached his cruiser at about the same time Merdon met his lieutenants in the dugout command post.

The Watchman spent only a few minutes in the cramped cubicle of his quarters. He stripped off his ragged clothes, ducked into the lav-stall for an automatic shower and air-blown drying, changed into a clean uniform and strapped on a sidearm. Then he left the cruiser and began to hunt for McIntyre.

The effect of the stimulant had reached its full force now, and would sustain Vorgens for several hours more. He felt strong and buoyant, his head was clear. He knew what he had to do, and although he was not particularly happy with the task ahead, he realized that it was the best possible alternative, under the circumstances.

As he searched through the welter of vehicles and equipment that comprised the Mobile Force, Vorgens could see that the men were ready for an attack at dawn. Hardly anyone was asleep. They were checking their weapons, taking stock of their supplies, making last-minute mechanical repairs on their battlewagons. Even the few that were stretched out on the decks and turrets were mostly wide-eyed and sleepless.

McIntyre was sitting in front of a cruiser, carefully adjusting the firing sight of a one-man missile launcher. He had to work with one hand, since his injured arm was still in the cast.

'Good morning sergeant.'

McIntyre looked up, then leaped to his feet, knocking the tubular missile launcher off its tripod.

'Sir! You made it back!'

Vorgens nodded curtly. 'I don't have much time for talking, Sergeant. I need volunteers – real volunteers.'

McIntyre's eyes widened as Vorgens explained what he intended to do, and the Star Watch regulations covering such situations.

'I'll need a dozen men. They should all be experienced, and they should be told exactly what they're getting into. Can you get me that many men in fifteen minutes?'

For the first time since Vorgens had known him, McIntyre seemed uncertain of himself. 'I can sure try, sir. I can sure try.'

It took closer to twenty minutes, but finally McIntyre had assembled a dozen men, noncoms and troopers, all of them. Vorgens looked them over as they lined up before the battle cruiser. They were a hard-faced, veteran crew.

'The sergeant has explained what this is about,' Vorgens told them. 'Although I am taking full responsibility for this action, there is a chance that your own records may receive a damaging report because of your help to me. If there is any man here who is afraid to run the risk of hurting his service record, he is free to fall out.'

None of the twelve moved. In fact, an extra man stepped out of the shadows and joined the tail end of the line.

'Giradaux!' McIntyre roared. 'Get outta there.'

The trooper's lean face twisted into a frown. 'Sarge, if you're in this, I want to be in on it, too. By glory, I'm a soldier, same as you.'

McIntyre stood before the youngster, his tall, thickset form looming over Giradaux' lanky frame. 'You're a soldier, all right, and when the wind's behind you, you're a bloody expedition. But this ain't soldiering, sonny, it's politics, and I'm gonna have enough to do without worryin' about you. Now fall out! *Move!*'

Giradaux stepped out of line, his face miserable. Vorgens walked over to him.

'I don't have time to explain,' the Watchman said, 'but the sergeant is trying to do you a favor. Don't feel disappointed.'

Without further ado, Vorgens marched his tiny contingent straight to Brigadier Aikens' dreadnaught. The sky was beginning to turn noticeably pink. There was precious little time left.

At the main hatch, Vorgens split up his men: 'You two take the communications center. You two, the engine compartment. Three of you take charge of the control center; three more, take the main turret. The remaining two will stay here at the hatch. Let no one in or out. Sergeant, you come with me.'

'You three headin' for the control center,' McIntyre instructed, 'make sure that all the other outside hatches are shut off.'

They clambered in through the hatch and hurried off to their assigned positions. Most of the dreadnaught's crew were in their bunks, and only a skeleton force was on hand to oppose Vorgens' armed men.

While the troopers seized control of the giant fighting vehicle, Vorgens and McIntyre marched to the exec's compartment. Vorgens knocked once and entered.

The exec was sitting on his bunk, with a writing table pulled across his lap. He looked up from the letter he was dictating into the audioprinter.

'What's wrong, Watchman?'

'Get your jacket on and come with me,' Vorgens ordered.

'What?'

'I don't have time for arguing. We're going to see the brigadier.'

'He'll throw you out . . .'

'No he won't. Put on your jacket and come. I'm sure the brigadier will want you as a witness.'

The exec pushed the writing table away and stood up. 'Witness? To what? What's going on here, Watchman?'

'You'll see soon enough. Come on.'

The exec grabbed his jacket from the rack over his bunk, then looked down at his bare feet.

'No time for putting on boots,' Vorgens said. 'Let's move.'

With a helpless shrug, the exec padded out into the passageway behind Vorgens, pulling on his jacket and buttoning it as they advanced to Brigadier Aikens' compartment.

Aikens, in full-dress uniform, was buckling a pair of ornate pistols across his middle when the door to his compartment abruptly opened. Vorgens and the exec stepped in. McIntyre remained out in the passageway.

'What on earth do you think you're doing?' Aikens bellowed. 'I told you to stay out of my sight, Watchman. What's the meaning of breaking in here like this? And you,' he turned to the exec, 'where are your boots?'

Vorgens said quietly, 'Brigadier Aikens, you are hereby

relieved of duty. I am assuming command of the Mobile Force.'

Aikens' mouth popped open, but for once in his life he was speechless. He simply stood there, his lips pursed into a silent, *Oh.*

'I realize that this is an unusual circumstance,' Vorgens continued, 'but the standard regulations clearly point out that all Imperial Marine personnel are subject to Star Watch jurisdiction.'

'But a junior officer can't assume command from a full brigadier,' the exec protested.

Vorgens smiled tightly. 'The regulations have no provision in them that prohibits such an action. I am the only Star Watch officer on this planet. I represent Star Watch Headquarters. I am not satisfied with Brigadier Aikens' handling of the situation, therefore, I must relieve him of duty. There is no one else to place in command but myself.'

'You're taking command of my Force?' Aikens rasped, finding his voice at last.

'This is not a decision I arrived at lightly, I assure you,' Vorgens said to the brigadier. 'I can see no alternative. I know this is unpleasant for you. It is equally unpleasant for me.'

'Unpleasant!' Aikens screamed. 'By all the gods of war, I'll have you shot before the sun comes up!' He began punching buttons on his desktop communicator.

Vorgens shook his head. 'I'm afraid that you'll find the dreadnaught is already under my command. I would appreciate it if you'd take off those guns and hand them over to me.'

For a stunned instant, Aikens stood frozen behind the desk. Then he slowly unbuckled the gunbelt and tossed it on the floor at Vorgens' feet. Vorgens waited for another explosion from the brigadier. Instead, the older man seemed more bewildered and uncomprehending than anything else. He sank down in his chair and stared ahead blankly.

Vorgens turned to the exec. 'We're going to break out of this valley. Inform all the officers that we will regroup immediately in Standard Formation 014. The breakout will be made in sectors W5 and W6. I want all units ready to move as soon as the sun clears the hills.'

The exec gasped. 'That's only ten or fifteen minutes from now.'

'Then you'll have to hurry.'

'Yes sir!'

The exec scampered out of the compartment, past McIntyre, headed for the communications center.

Vorgens turned back to the brigadier. 'I'm sorry it had to happen this way, sir. But I really have no other choice. I was sent to Shinar to try to arrange a truce. Now it is apparent that my first job is to prevent the Komani from destroying this Force, because if they are successful against us, a new galactic war will be triggered. That must be avoided at all costs. Surely you can see that.'

'I can see that you're trying to ruin me,' Aikens said dully. 'You're trying to destroy a record of fifty-five years of service with your own half-cocked dreams of glory.'

'That's not true at all,' Vorgens countered. 'Ever since I came to Shinar, I've been shunted around from place to place by you, by the Komani, by some of the Shinarians. I've been pushed into killing some of the people with whom I came to negotiate. I've been turned into a messenger boy. I've been taken prisoner, and had a death sentence read over me. I've been rescued from a firing squad by an old man and a girl, because they saw in me what I had almost forgotten was there – a chance to bring peace to Shinar, to prevent this war from starting.

'Now I've stopped playing messenger. I'm a Star Watch officer, and I'm going to take the responsibility that goes with the uniform. I've seen the enemy face to face, and I've seen the rebels, too. Fighting, killing, destroying – that's not going to bring peace to this planet. I've got to convince the rebels of this.'

Aikens grunted. 'And the Komani? Are you going to talk them out of their plans of conquest?'

'No, I'm afraid not. They will pay attention only to force. But when we fight them, I want it to be on *my* terms, at a time and place that *I* chose, not at Okatar's convenience.'

Aikens' eyes glittered with rage. 'If – I say, *if*, Watchman – if we both live through this, I'm going to see you before the highest military tribunal in the Empire, stripped of rank and uniform, and sentenced to the worst penalty they can mete out.'

'Perhaps,' Vorgens said, 'Perhaps.' Then he added softly, 'But the first thing we must do is live through today, isn't it?'

Vorgens dropped to one knee and picked up the brigadier's pistol belt. Then the Watchman straightened to attention and made a formal salute to Aikens. The older man did not return the salute, but merely sat behind his desk, glaring at Vorgens.

The Star Watchman left the compartment. McIntyre was still standing out in the passageway.

'Get one of your men,' Vorgens said, as he shut the brigadier's door, 'to stand watch at this post. Then join me at the control center.'

'Yes sir,' McIntyre said, with a salute. Then he relaxed for a moment and said, with a grin, 'Congratulations, sir. And good luck.'

Vorgens returned the smile. 'Thank you, sergeant. We'll need all the luck we can get.'

The control center was a half-level above the officers' quarters, and just under the dreadnaught's main turret. Like every compartment in the mammoth groundcar, the control deck was cramped and low-ceilinged. In addition, it was crammed with computer units, communications equipment, and a tight semicircle of control desks, where tech-specialists could keep in constant touch with every part of the vehicle, and with every vehicle in the Mobile Force.

Vorgens climbed up the ladder from the level below, and silently took the commander's seat at the half-circle of control desks. In the dim, greenish light from the viewscreens he could see that most of the crew was uncertain, anxious. The battle was about to begin, and a new, totally untried commander was in charge.

'I want my instructions processed automatically by the master computer and relayed immediately to the rest of the Force,' Vorgens said quietly.

The computer and communications men nodded and began setting up their instruments to carry out the Star Watchman's commands.

'Computer ready, sir,' called out the tech-specialist.
'Communications ready, sir.'

95

Vorgens nodded. On the desk before him, he could see a pair of green lights signaling what the men had just told him.

For a moment, he hesitated. Looking up at the men around him – all of them staring back at him – Vorgens suddenly realized that every one of them was a complete stranger. Even McIntyre he had known for less than a week.

With an abrupt shake of his head, Vorgens put such thoughts aside. He began dictating his instructions.

Deep in the bowels of the dreadnaught, the master computer translated the Star Watchman's words into electromagnetic pulses and began sorting them out with the speed of light. Automatically, the computer processed the instructions into a separate set of orders for each of the three hundred individual vehicles in the Mobile Force.

Automatically, each set of orders was relayed to the communications transmitter and beamed to each individual dreadnaught, cruiser, scoutcar, troopcarrier, supply van. On three hundred separate vehicles, communications receivers relayed the messages to computers. On three hundred vehicles, computers suddenly chugged to life and busily rattled off detailed orders. As the tapes wormed out of the printers three hundred skippers read the orders and began barking commands. The sum total of all these individual messages was Vorgens' plan for breaking out of the Komani trap.

Scoutcars and troopcarriers were to speed to the slopes where the Komani had thinned out their forces – Sectors W5 and W6 on the Terran maps. The troopers were to seize those two sectors and hold them, with the scoutcars neutralizing any pockets of enemy resistance. Light cruisers, slower and less maneuverable than the smaller vehicles, would follow up the first assault and provide extra firepower.

As the troopers gained command of the slopes, engineers' vans were to immediately begin grading the territory, using force beams and explosives. The objective was to gouge out a broad, easy slope with no major obstructions, so that the larger vehicles of the Mobile Force could skim up the slopes and out of the valley as quickly as possible. Vorgens remembered how his battle cruiser was forced to crawl along the twisting, narrow trail up the slopes. He wanted no more of that. If the entire Mobile Force had to file out of the valley like that, they would never escape alive.

While the troopers were holding open the escape route and the engineers were making it ready to handle the main body of the Mobile Force, the rest of the Force was to fall back slowly toward the escape slopes. A special task unit of ten dreadnaughts, including Vorgens' flagship, was to form a rear guard, and to keep the Komani attack stalled and off balance until the final dash for freedom.

'That's the plan,' Vorgens muttered to himself as he watched the computer's steady stream of orders flash across the viewscreen at his elbow. 'Now to see if it will work.'

CHAPTER ELEVEN

BREAKOUT

Okatar Kang stood at the crest of a hill with the first rays of the rising sun at his back. Below him, the valley floor was still cloaked in darkness, but the Komani technicians had set up a battery of viewscreens that showed the Mobile Force.

The Kang paced restlessly behind the technicians, who were seated before their mobile viewscreens. The high-pitched shriek of Terran engines was wafting up from the valley.

'What are they doing?' Okatar demanded of no one in particular.

One of his nobles, pacing alongside him, answered, 'They are preparing for the battle, starting their engines.'

The viewscreens suddenly went blank. Before Okatar could say anything, the technicians had readjusted them, and the pictures of the sprawling Terran armored Force reappeared.

'They've put up an energy shield,' one of the technicians said.

'We expected that,' said the noble at Okatar's elbow. 'It cannot be a very powerful shield, since its generating equipment must be small and mobile. An hour's worth of force beams should saturate it.'

'What about missiles?' Okatar snapped.

'The Terran shield will probably stop some of them, but not all. Their shield could not possibly be as strong as the screen we have around our camp. Of course, our warriors will be able to penetrate the shield with ease. Not even the Terrans have been able to devise an energy screen so solid that a man cannot step through it.'

Okatar nodded. 'How much longer before the signal?'

The noble glanced at the watch set into his jeweled wristband. 'The signal should be given – *now*.'

A hundred beams of light lanced out of the hills down toward the still-shadowy valley floor and splashed into blinding brilliance against the Terran energy shield. Missiles roared through the morning mists and exploded in flashes of flame. Through the noise of the explosion rose a mighty shout as Komani warriors charged down from the hilltops, riding their one-man flyers straight toward the Terrans.

Okatar stood riveted before the viewscreens, his nobles clustered about him. They watched the Terran armored vehicles shift positions as they awaited the onslaught of the Komani. Here and there, missiles penetrated the Mobile Force's energy shield and blasted into the ground. One of them hit a cruiser, and Okatar could not restrain an exultant laugh. The force beams, though, were stopped completely by the shield.

'What are they up to?' Okatar wondered aloud as he watched the screens.

The smallest Terran vehicles – scoutcars and troop carriers – seemed headed for the rear, while the big dreadnaughts and battle cruisers were moving up to face the Komani attack.

'They're moving their lightly armored vehicles away from our missile barrage,' one of the nobles said.

Okatar looked up from the screen. It was light enough now to see the valley floor clearly. The Komani warriors were halfway down the hills, halfway to the valley floor. But his attack was not interesting Okatar as much as the Terrans' moves toward the rear.

'Why are they pulling their troops away from the fighting? Do they expect to face my warriors with their armored vehicles alone, without infantry support?'

'The Terrans have no stomach for facing our warriors man to man,' said a noble. 'They are too cowardly to fight, except from within an armored vehicle.'

Okatar nodded, but his face was still frowning in puzzlement.

At his slot in the control center, Vorgens watched the viewscreen before him, his high forehead puckered into worried wrinkles.

Someone slid into the empty seat next to him. Vorgens looked up. It was the exec.

The older officer smiled, 'Reports from Sector W5 and 6

sound pretty smooth so far. Everything progressing according to plan. Light resistance.'

'Are the engineers ready to go?' Vorgens asked. 'That's the most critical part of the operation.'

'Ready and anxious. As soon as you give the word.'

Vorgens nodded. 'Where's Sergeant McIntyre?'

'I believe he went out with the other troopers in the vans.'

'Yes, that sounds like him.'

The Star Watchman returned his attention to the viewscreen. It was bright daylight now, so that the infra-red scanners were no longer necessary. The screen showed the hills before them, with the glaring, yellow Oran automatically filtered out. Flashes from force beams blazed almost continuously against the energy shield now, and explosions churned up the valley floor. The mammoth dreadnaughts and battle cruisers were weaving back and forth in an intricate, computer-controlled dance that had so far kept the Komani missiles limited to two damaging hits and a half-dozen minor ones. Anti-missiles were picking off a good many incoming missiles, as well. So far the Komani had not used nuclear warheads. Probably they only had a few and were saving them for an emergency, Vorgens thought, or for the moment when the energy screen collapsed.

The Watchman's attention was focused on the Komani warriors making their way on their one-man flyers down the broken, tumbled rocks toward the valley floor. They were about halfway between the crest of the hills and the bottom.

'They're sticking pretty close to cover,' the exec observed.

'Yes, but the cover thins out rather quickly as they approach the valley floor,' Vorgens said. 'I think we can hold our fire for another few minutes, and then hit them with a massed barrage.'

The exec nodded agreement. 'We might try peppering the hilltops with missiles, too. The Komani probably have their second and third waves up there.'

Vorgens thought a moment. 'I'd rather wait until I see some definite targets. No sense wasting ammunition on probabilities.'

'As you wish.'

And no sense bombarding the Shinarian rebels, Vorgens thought to himself, *if we can avoid getting them into combat altogether*.

100

'What's the latest word from W5 and 6?' the Watchman asked.

The exec flicked a switch on his desk communicator, and scanned the report that flashed across its tiny viewscreen. 'The troopers have advanced about halfway up the slopes. Their perimeter is almost exactly as planned – the outer edges of the two sectors. Looks good.'

'Start the engineers to work.'

'Yes sir.' The exec pressed a stud on the communicator.

'Are all the units in the forward battle line ready to fire?' Vorgens asked.

'All units report fire control tracking and standing by,' answered the communications tech.

Vorgens took a last look at the viewscreen before him. The Komani warriors were nearing the base of the hills.

'Commence firing.'

The Terran battle line let loose a devastating hail of beams and missiles that caught the advanced elements of the Komani attackers in an inescapable deluge of fire. The force beams sprayed back and forth across the lines of warriors and their little flyers. Men and machines were sliced apart, brush and grass set ablaze, rocks and earth vaporized by the intense beams of light. Anti-personnel missiles exploded overhead, showering the area with deadly shrapnel.

The spearhead of the Komani attack was shattered. The Terran curtain of fire began to creep up the face of the hills, catching the Komani warriors further back. The Komani advance halted and the warriors took whatever cover they could find among the sparse bushes and jagged rocks of the hillsides.

'We stopped them!' the exec marveled. 'Stopped them cold.'

'Too easily,' Vorgens countered.

'We could counterattack; move up those hills and mop them up.'

Vorgens shook his head. 'Perhaps that's what they expect us to do. No, instead of attacking, we're moving back. Pass the word – all units to fall back slowly half a mile.'

'But that will give us less room for maneuvering – make us a more compact target.'

'Yes, and it will also make a greater open space between

us and the enemy; an open space almost completely without cover. This is a rearguard action, remember. We're trying to avoid major contact with the enemy.'

The exec nodded, then began giving out the necessary orders on his communicator.

Slowly, the ponderous dreadnaughts and cruisers and their escorting vehicles began to withdraw from their positions. The battlewagons on the flanks pulled back first, then those in the center joined in the movement. A huge bowed line, spreading nearly the width of the valley floor, edged backward, away from the still-rising sun.

They were in the midst of the maneuver when the *real* Komani attack came howling out of the hills on both their flanks. Thousands of warriors swarmed down on both sides of the Terran line and began pouring fire into the armored vehicles.

'This is it,' Vorgens muttered as he watched his viewscreen. The hills, even the sky, seemed black with charging Komani.

'Good grief, look at them,' the exec said. 'It's a lucky thing we didn't advance when I wanted to. We'd have been surrounded.'

'Let's get to work,' Vorgens said.

The Watchman began dictating a steady stream of orders. In response, the Terran battle line continued to edge backward, and bowed even more, with the battlewagons on both flanks pulling back further and facing outward to meet the double attack of the Komani.

A sudden hail of missiles and force beams, including a few nuclear missiles, smashed into the Terran forces. One of the nuclear warheads got through and vaporized a dreadnaught. Vorgens' own vehicle, a few stations up the line, bucked and rattled when the concussion wave blew past.

As abruptly as it came, the Komani barrage ended, and the flying warriors swarmed into the massed Terran vehicles. Vorgens met them with concentrated fire, his dreadnaughts and cruisers sweeping the sky with force beams.

Despite frightful losses, the warriors continued to bore in. They penetrated the energy shield, and began attacking individual vehicles with grenades and missile-guns. Vorgens ordered his vehicles to 'pop hatches' and allow the crews to meet the attackers with handguns and rifles – much more effective now than the powerful, long-range weapons in the turrets.

The main batteries of the dreadnaughts and cruisers, at Vorgens' orders, kept up a constant rain of fire on the slopes of the hills, in an effort to prevent the Komani from reinforcing their first wave of attackers.

The battle line of Terran armor was enveloped in a wild, confused struggle of men and machines. Komani warriors swooped everywhere, shooting and bombing as they flew. Terran Marines crouched in their hatches and fought back with force beams and anti-personnel missiles and grenades. The big turrets spat their beams of death toward the hills while the smaller gun batteries aboard the battlewagons spun and fired at the darting Komani warriors. Dust and smoke, explosions and flame, enveloped everyone and everything.

Deep within his dreadnaught, at the control center, Vorgens could hear the muffled explosions as his eyes watched the battle shift back and forth, on the viewscreen.

'We've got to disengage from the warriors,' he muttered to himself. 'We've got to scrape them off our backs . . . otherwise the whole plan will fail.'

Okatar Kang stood under the cloudless sky and watched the raging battle on the valley floor. He ignored the viewscreens set up before him, and instead held a pair of molectronic binoculars to his eyes. When he put them down, his face was set in a grim mask of anger.

One of the nobles standing beside him said, 'The warriors have penetrated the Terran energy shield on both flanks. It is only a matter of time now. Shall I have the Shinarians join the attack?'

'They have no transport. It will take them the better part of an hour before they can reach the fighting,' Okatar grumbled.

'Then we had better start them now.'

'Yes, send them off.' Okatar paced along the crest of the hill. The breeze was blowing down from the higher hills toward the valley floor, so that the smoke and noise of the battle was carried away from him.

'Why did they retreat?' Okatar demanded. 'The frontal

attack did not fool them. They did not hold their ground. They retreated. Why? Did they know that we would attack their flanks? If they had advanced, or even held their ground, our double flank attack would have overwhelmed them. Now – the issue is in doubt.'

'Their commander made a lucky guess,' one of the nobles answered. 'Our men will still prevail over them.'

'But at what cost? Our losses will be very heavy.'

'For every man who falls today,' another noble predicted, 'a hundred Komani warriors will join your standards tomorrow. This victory will establish you as the leader of all the clans, everywhere.'

Okatar looked hard at the noble. 'If we have a victory today.'

'Surely you don't think that the Terrans could defeat us!'

'Not of themselves,' Okatar replied. 'But we have traitors in our camp. Men in whom our trust is misplaced. Perhaps ...'

A communications technician jumped up from his field table and dashed over to the Kang.

'What is it?' Okatar demanded.

The tech bowed quickly and answered, 'Reports from our men holding the far hills, on the other side of the valley, sire. They have been under attack since the sun rose, and steadily forced back. If they are not reinforced, the Terrans will drive them from their positions and open an escape lane out of the valley.'

Okatar snapped his binoculars to his eyes. 'By the blood of our forefathers,' he thundered, 'the smoke is covering the area completely.'

A noble shrugged at the news. 'A Terran diversion. They cannot possibly get those lumbering vehicles of theirs across the hills in any time less than a day. There are no roads, and no trails wider than—'

'Sire, the Terran engineers are blasting out roadbeds through the area that our warriors have been driven from.'

Okatar roared something unintelligible and thrust the startled technician aside. He strode to the communications table and talked directly to the leader of the Komani under attack.

When Okatar straightened up and faced his nobles, his

face was furious. 'They're seizing the hills and building an escape road through them. If we don't stop them, they'll be out of this valley before nightfall.'

'But how . . .'

'How did they know that those particular hills were held with only a skeleton force? Who told them?'

'Sire, we can find the traitors later. At the moment we must prevent the Terrans from escaping.'

'Contact the second and third waves of our attacking forces and order them to close the gap in our lines in those hills.'

'But – what about the main attack?'

'The first wave alone will have to do as much damage to the Terrans as it can,' Okatar said. 'Have the warriors who made the original frontal attack join them.'

'What about the Shinarians?'

'Get them into the battle as quickly as they can get there. But I doubt that they will be in time.'

The oldest noble of the group, his facial hair grizzled and his back bent with years, spoke up. 'Sire, you are condemning the brave warriors of the first attacking wave to certain death. They cannot destroy the Terran forces by themselves, without support.'

Okatar nodded curtly. 'They will buy time for us, while we sew up the trap again. The Terrans must not escape, no matter what the price. That is my command!'

As he sat in the control center, watching the progress of the see-saw battle over his armored vehicles, Vorgens felt a cold, hard knot forming in his stomach. He had taken the responsibility of command, and now the anxiety and tension of that burden were making themselves felt.

'What time is it?' he asked.

'Almost noon,' the exec replied.

'It's not going too well, is it?'

'We're holding our own.'

'But we've got to disengage from this attack. We can't retreat, or try to support the troopers up in the hills, while the Komani are on top of us.'

The exec rubbed his jaw for a moment. 'Listen,' he said, 'each vehicle has a complement of armored flying suits. Why don't we form a reserve brigade and throw them at the Komani? Maybe we could clear them off.'

Vorgens nodded. 'It's worth a try.'

As the exec began rattling off the orders to form a flying reserve brigade, Vorgens suddenly felt the strength ebbing out of him. His head began to throb, it was an effort to raise his arm and rub his forehead, even his vision seemed to be going blurry.

Energy capsule, he said to himself, as he fumbled with his tunic pocket. *Need another booster.*

He pulled the two remaining pills from the pocket and stared at them in the palm of his hand for a blank moment. Then he realized a noncom was at his elbow with a cup of water.

'Thank you,' Vorgens mumbled, and he took one of the capsules.

'Anything else, sir?' the noncom asked.

Vorgens looked up at the Terran. He was as young as the Watchman himself, pink-cheeked, bright-eyed, without the weight of the galaxy's peace on his shoulders.

'No, that's all, thanks ... Or wait – remind me in six hours to take the other pill.'

'Certainly, sir.'

Vorgens focused his attention back on the viewscreen. The battle was still raging outside the dreadnaught. Several vehicles were ablaze now, and the ground between them was bomb-pitted and littered with dead and dying men, both Terran and Komani.

'The flying squads are ready to go, sir.'

Vorgens squeezed his eyes shut and tried to think. 'It would probably be better if they massed at one spot, and then hit the Komani as a solid unit. Don't you think so?'

The exec nodded. 'Exactly. I've given them the word to group first at battle cruiser J-7' – he pointed to the stereo-map on the desktop before him – 'in the middle of our battle line.'

'Good. Have them sweep to the far side of the valley first, and once that flank is cleared, they can come back this way.'

'Right.' The exec flicked a switch on his communicator and gave the orders.

From every vehicle of the embattled Terran group, a half-dozen or so men emerged, clad in armored suits with jetbelts on their backs. Some of them never cleared the hatches: Komani warriors cut them down. But most of them fought their way toward the rendezvous point over a flame-blackened, battered cruiser, and then wheeled as a unit and began advancing on the milling, free-wheeling Komani attackers.

The Komani warriors fought mostly as single units. That was their glory and their strength. Their tactics were chaos and confusion. They merely blackened the sky and hit their enemy from every direction at once.

But the Terran flying brigade had the solidity and firepower of an airborne dreadnaught. Like a mammoth cloud of death, the Terrans began sweeping the sky clean of the Komani.

Vorgens watched the progress of the aerial battle. But a corner of his mind refused to devote itself to the struggle overhead. Something was out of place. Something had changed in the picture on his viewscreen. What was it?

The main batteries of the dreadnaughts and cruisers were no longer firing into the hills, as he had ordered! But some of the battlewagons were shooting missiles and force beams across the valley floor, in the direction where the first attack had come from, at sunrise.

What's going on? Vorgens wondered.

The Star Watchman began twisting the control knobs of his viewscreen, in an effort to get a panoramic view of all the action.

Komani warriors were advancing along the valley floor, from the same spot where the sunrise attack had started.

But that was just a holding attack, meant to draw us into the trap on our flanks.

And on those flanks, where the Komani should be pouring wave after wave of attackers – nothing. Silence. No enemy action.

The main attack was coming from our flanks, Vorgens reasoned. *Now Okatar has stopped that attack. He's left his men here over our vehicles, with no further support.*

The answer flashed into his mind with blinding clarity. At the same moment, a trio of nuclear explosions rocked the summit of the hills where the Terran troopers and engineers were struggling to open up an escape route.

'The enemy has broken off his attack on us,' Vorgens shouted into the exec's ear. 'They're trying to recapture Sectors W5 and 6!'

The exec arched his eyebrows and punched a button on his communicator. A report lit up on his viewscreen.

'The troopers have taken the crest of the hills. The engineers have blasted out a passable grade about a third of the way up to the top . . . Hold on, there's more. The troopers are under bombardment. Looks as though a major counterattack is on the way.'

'Get every cruiser out of this battle line and up those hills as fast as possible,' Vorgens snapped. 'Put every available man from the dreadnaughts into flying suits and clear the attackers off our decks. I want nothing but skeleton crews aboard the dreadnaughts. We've got an escape route open. Now it's going to be a race to hold it!'

Sergeant McIntyre wormed through the brush, a pistol in his good hand, and took a careful look out over the edge of the ridge. Down below, a hundred yards or so, a squad of Komani were setting up a heavy beamgun to spray the ridge where McIntyre's men had dug in.

The Terran troopers had won that ridge in midmorning against stiff Komani resistance, and had held it against three counterattacks of steadily increasing fury.

The Terrans had dug in and waited for the engineers, and finally the main body of the Mobile Force, to reach them. But now, late in the afternoon, they had seen nothing but enemy warriors.

A missile shrieked by. McIntyre instinctively dug his face into the grassy ground. The blinding flash, instantly followed by an ear-splitting explosion, told him that another nuclear warhead had been fired at them. Fully half the men he had started out with were already dead or wounded, but that particular missile, McIntyre knew, was off target. It plowed up some ground, knocked down trees for a square mile around, and sent up an ugly mushroom cloud, but it hadn't hit any of his men. If anything, it had merely made the engineers' job a little easier by clearing some more of the hilly country for them.

Patiently, McIntyre waited until the Komani squad had

put their beamgun together. Then he tossed a pair of grenades at them, in rapid succession. The explosions were sharp but unspectacular. When the smoke cleared, the beamgun was a shambles and the Komani killed. With a grim smile of satisfaction, McIntyre edged back to the slit trench where Giradaux and the rest of his men were waiting.

Another strong attack'll finish us, the sergeant knew. *And th' Komani are gettin' set for a big one. Pretty soon now. Plenty of movement down in that brush. They're just about set to wipe us up.*

Someone was rushing toward him, racing as fast as he could while doubled over so that one hand nearly touched the ground. McIntyre pointed his pistol at the lanky, awkward form, then recognized Giradaux.

'I thought I told you to stay with the others,' the sergeant growled as Giradaux flopped belly down beside him.

'We got a visitor back at the trench, Sarge. An engineer.' Giradaux's lean, angular face was split by a big toothy grin. 'Say's he's got a couple of cruisers crawling up right behind him, and the dreadnaughts are on their way, too!'

McIntyre looked at the grinning trooper, then suddenly scrambled to his feet. Standing bolt upright, he stared down toward the valley floor.

About twenty Terran vehicles were scattered across the valley, smoking and inert. The rest of the Mobile Force was streaming up the hillsides, along paths of raw earth gouged out by the engineers and the Komani bombardment, toward the crest of the hills – toward freedom.

Giradaux and the sergeant scampered back to the slit trench. A battle-scarred cruiser was already there, and the troopers were clambering aboard its rear deck.

'He did it!' McIntyre shouted to the young trooper. 'That Star Watchman has pulled us outta the trap. We're gettin' outta this valley – alive!'

The engineer, grimy and hollow-eyed, called from his one-man scoutcar, 'No time for celebration, sergeant. Let's get out of here before the Komani try to hit us again.'

McIntyre grabbed a handhold on the cruiser's side and hoisted himself upwards.

'They ain't gonna try anything now,' he answered, over his shoulder. 'They've lost this battle, and they know it.'

The cruiser whined into life, lifted off the ground by

about a foot, and rumbled off with the battered, jubilant troopers aboard. The engineer gunned his little scrambler and scooted up alongside, placing the cruiser between himself and the Komani.

Half a mile away, a Komani officer stood under a cloudy, smoke-filled sky and spoke into his wrist communicator:

'The main body of the Terran forces has reached the summit of the hills. We will attack again if you order us to, but my company is down to less than half its original strength. The Terrans have the advantage of massed firepower, and their armored vehicles are faster than our flyers, once they are in open country.'

After a long wait, an utterly exhausted voice sounded from the communicator, 'Break off contact with the enemy. Regroup your men. The battle is over.'

CHAPTER TWELVE

SITTAS

It showered briefly at sunset, as the Mobile Force streamed out to the rolling, open countryside. Then all through the night clouds piled up thicker and darker until, by dawn, it began to rain steadily.

Sittas heard the first drops strike the roof over his head. The old priest was standing by a window on the upper floor of the town hall of Matara, a tiny farming village a few miles from the valley of Carmeer.

He had turned the town hall – the only two-storey building in the village – into an emergency hospital. Terrans, Komani, and the few Shinarians who had been wounded in the battle were being brought in. Sittas stood by the window after a full night of dressing wounds and blessing the dead, and watched the maimed and shattered men still being brought through the muddy, rain-spattered morning into the makeshift infirmary. When would the pitiful parade end? Sittas had gathered every doctor and every available boy and woman from miles around. But they were few, terribly few, for this horrible toll.

'It's not a very pretty sight, is it?'

Sittas turned and saw Altai at the door, a raincape over her shoulders, her hair glistening wet.

'You are . . . all right?'

She nodded. 'The Watchman kept his word. The Terrans avoided firing on us. Only Merdon and his best three squads got into the fighting, and they had to ride piggy-back on Komani flyers to reach the Terrans. Merdon could have stayed out of it altogether. The Watchman gave us that opportunity.'

'Well, thank heaven that you are safe, and that more of our people were not involved in the battle. Merdon was not hurt, was he?'

'No, he's all right.'

'Good.'

Altai stepped over to the window and looked at the steady line of wounded coming into the building.

'It was an awful battle, though. Even if our people didn't have much to do with it.'

'I know,' the priest said. 'Unless we can bring peace to Shinar quickly, this will be only the first of many, many battles, and our people will be fully involved in the next ones.'

'What do you intend to do?' she asked.

Sittas shook his head. 'I'm not certain. That's the terrible part of it. I don't know what to do next.'

'You're tired,' Altai said. 'We all are. Time to sleep now.'

'But the wounded need help . . .'

She took him by the arm and steered him to a couch along the far wall of the room. 'The wounded don't need someone who's about to fall asleep on them. Sleep now, and you'll be much better able to help them when you awake.'

The old man sat on the edge of the couch. 'You remind me very much of my sister . . . your mother. She was very domineering, too, despite being much younger than I.'

Altai smiled at him. 'Enough talking. Sleep,' she said firmly.

With a resigned shrug, Sittas kicked off his sandals and stretched out on the couch. Altai put her raincape over him, and walked softly out of the room. The lights went off as she closed the door.

Squatting outside in the pelting rain, a Komani warrior eyed the town-hall-turned-hospital with the patient cunning of a stalking panther. The old man is in there, the warrior knew. Only the wounded, or Shinarian doctors and helpers, were allowed inside. Sooner or later the old man would come out. Then the warrior would kill him. Time did not matter. The reason behind the warrior's orders did not matter. All the warrior knew was that Sittas must die. There was no other purpose for the Komani's existence but to carry out the order of death. Silently he sat in the rain, his chin cupped in his massive hands, and waited.

Sittas was awakened by the sounds of three Shinarian

youths trying to place a wounded Komani on a makeshift pallet of blankets and coats. The town hall was overflowing. The rain had stopped, and a late afternoon sun was slanting through the windows. Outside, Sittas could see that more wounded had been left on litters in the town square.

The old priest immediately went downstairs, into the welter of cots and pallets and doctors and weary, busy women and boys who were attending the injured men. Altai was among them.

'Here,' Sittas said to his niece, as she tried to wrap a bandage over a young Terran's arm. 'I'll do that. You find the town mayor and bring him here immediately.'

The mayor was short, round and bland-faced. He listened patiently as Sittas explained what he wanted to do, then replied with a shrug:

'The people probably won't want to bring wounded foreigners into their homes, but I shall tell them that you have asked them to do so. We shall see how they react.'

The reaction was startling, even to Sittas. Nearly every family in the tiny village showed up at the town square and took at least one of the wounded men lying out on the worn old paving stones. The casualties were all safely indoors before night fell.

The mayor was amazed. 'These people revere you, Sittas.'

The priest shook his head. 'It is not me. They are good-hearted people. I only pointed out how they could help.'

All through the night, with only an hour or so of rest, Sittas attended 'his' patients. Near dawn, one of the doctors reported worriedly:

'We have just about stripped the entire district clean of medical supplies. There's practically nothing left to go on.'

Altai, standing nearby her uncle, said, 'Perhaps I can get more.'

As she went off toward the building's only tri-di transceiver, a Komani officer strode into the main entrance. He looked across the sea of bedridden men that filled the entryway and stretched on into the other rooms.

'Which of you is in charge here?' he demanded of the Shinarians.

Everyone turned toward Sittas.

'I am Sittas,' the priest said, making his way toward the Komani. He saw a trio of warriors standing just outside the doorway.

The Komani officer said, 'In the name of Okatar Kang, I claim the Terrans sheltered here as prisoners . . .'

'Never!' Sittas snapped, with a vehemence that surprised them all.

The old man walked up to the Komani, and, standing barely as tall as the officer's breastbone, said furiously, 'This place is sanctuary for wounded men. Do you understand? Sanctuary. Neither Okatar Kang nor the Terran commander has any right to claim prisoners here. The men here are no longer warriors – not until they are well enough to rejoin their companions. In this town the war does not exist. Isn't it enough that you have killed and crippled so many? Get out of here – you smell of death. Out!'

The Komani officer was forced back a step. Uncertainly, he mumbled, 'Well, if it's sanctuary . . . we have no quarrel with your religious feelings.' He turned and walked out. The three warriors followed him.

Outside, the Komani warrior who had been silently waiting for almost three days, sat immobile and watched the entrance to the town hall. For an instant Sittas was framed in the doorway, and the warrior's hand slid to the butt of his pistol, but then the priest turned away and went back inside the building. The warrior grunted to himself and relaxed. He did not stop watching.

News of sporadic fighting between the Terrans and Komani trickled into the hospital that morning. The Mobile Force was in the open country, and a few of their scoutcars had brushed briefly with Komani patrols.

Near noontime a Terran supply van rumbled through the dusty main street of Matara and stopped before the town hall. A white flag flew from its whip antenna. A lieutenant and five other Marines got out of the cab and entered the building, looking for Sittas.

'We have a van full of medical supplies, sir,' the lieutenant told the priest. 'Compliments of the Terran Imperial Star Watch and Marine Corps.'

As the Terrans, with a dozen Shinarian youths helping them, unloaded the supplies, Sittas found Altai and said:

'I know this is your doing. But how did you accomplish it?'

She smiled at her uncle. 'I phoned our people in Capital City. They saw to it that the Terran garrison there learned of your need for medical help. The garrison informed the Star Watchman, I suppose, and he sent the supplies.'

Sittas shook his head. 'Lines of communication become very strange in wartime.'

Before the Terran van was unloaded completely, a small civilian groundcar pulled up beside it. The driver hopped out lightly, trotted around to the passenger's side, and opened the door. A tall, broad-girthed, balding Shinarian stepped out – Clanthas.

He cocked an eye at the Terran vehicle, then walked into the town hall. For several minutes he spoke to no one, but merely paced slowly through the improvised hospital, watching Shinarians tending the wounded Terrans and Komani. He nodded to a few of the doctors, grinned at the women and youths assisting them.

Finally, Clanthas spotted Sittas. The old priest was standing on the balcony that ran around three sides of the large, ground-level room that had been the town hall's main auditorium. Clanthas climbed the stairs slowly, yet he was still puffing a bit when he reached the top.

Sittas was locked in a discussion with one of the doctors.

'All right, they're well enough to leave and rejoin the rest of the Terrans,' the doctor was saying. 'But how do you get them back to their own men safely, without the Komani stopping them?'

'We can put them on the Terran van, outside,' Sittas replied.

'And what about tomorrow, or the day after?'

'We can ask the Terrans leaving today to have their commander keep in touch with us by tri-di. When we are ready to release more of them, they can send another vehicle, under a truce flag.'

'And you expect the Komani to honor the flag of truce?'

Sittas nodded. 'They know that their own wounded are being tended here. If they do anything to disrupt our work, their own men will suffer for it.'

The doctor shrugged. 'I hope you're right . . . Very well.

115

I'll tell the Terran lieutenant that we'll have a few men for him to take back with him.'

'Good.'

As the doctor turned to find the lieutenant, Clanthas stepped up to the old priest.

'You do not know me. My name is Clanthas.'

Sittas' wrinkled face broke into a smile. 'Clanthas of Katan? The merchant who organized the first protests and demonstrations against the Terrans?'

Clanthas nodded, with a rueful grin. 'I did help to get the movement started; it has gone much farther than I expected.'

'Yes. But your aims and ideals were good ones. I am honored to meet you.'

'Thank you.'

'You are looking for your son, Merdon? He is not here, but he is well and happy.'

'Yes, I know. I spoke with Merdon on tri-di last night. Actually, I came here to see you, and this hospital. News of what you have done is spreading all over Shinar. You have become a national hero, Sittas.'

'Me?' Sittas laughed. 'An unlikely hero, I must say. I have done practically nothing. It is the doctors, and the good people of this town. And the Terran commander, too; he sent us a van-load of medical supplies.'

'Yes, I know. My driver parked next to the Terran van. Fortunately, they don't know who I am.'

Altai hurried up the stairs to her uncle. 'Excuse me. The Terrans have finished unloading. Their lieutenant wants to speak with you.'

'Ah yes; and there are several things I want to talk over with him.' Sittas turned back to Clanthas. 'Will you pardon me for a moment?'

'Certainly.'

The priest gestured toward the girl. 'My niece, Altai, will be glad to show you around the building and to answer any questions you may have. Altai, this is Clanthas of Katan, Merdon's father.'

'Merdon's father?' Altai gasped as Sittas started down the stairs. Her hands flew to her hair. 'I . . . I must look terrible. These slacks and this old blouse . . . you must excuse my appearance, I had no idea . . .'

Clanthas chuckled at her. 'I wasn't expecting to find you in a ball gown. Merdon has told me quite a bit about you. You are as lovely as he said you were.'

'Oh . . . thank you.'

They began to talk, mostly about Merdon, and were deep in conversation when Sittas returned.

'I have decided to accompany the Terrans back to the Mobile Force,' the old man said. 'The lieutenant has told me that the Star Watchman has assumed command of all Terran units on Shinar. He has asked to see me, and I believe it might be helpful to go to him, now that he has such power in his hands.'

'I've heard some rumors about a Watchman on the planet,' Clanthas said. 'You know him?'

Sittas nodded. 'Altai can tell you about it. I must hurry off, the Terrans are anxious to leave.'

The old priest, flanked by the Terran lieutenant and five troopers, left the building and climbed into the cab of the bulky supply van. The Komani warrior who had been waiting in the town square watched with helpless fury. He could not get a good shot at the old man with six Terrans surrounding him, and he could not get close enough to use a grenade without the Terrans stopping him.

As the supply van whined to life and lifted off the pavement, the Komani wearily trudged back to his own flyer, resting in an alley off the square. Perhaps he could catch up with the van in the open country. If the Terrans were not alert, he could execute the old man, and get a half-dozen Terrans in the bargain.

CHAPTER THIRTEEN

VORGENS

Sittas eyed the Star Watchman critically as they sat in the tiny compartment aboard the dreadnaught. The priest had never before been inside a vehicle of such size, yet he was most amazed at how much the Terrans were able to squeeze into the big groundcar.

Vorgens' quarters, where they were sitting, was typical. The bunk was folded into the bulkhead; the webbed chairs and table had been slid out of the same opening that the bunk fitted into. The short side of the compartment was taken up with a translucent viewscreen, another wall had a stereomap scanner built into it. The furniture was stored in the third wall, and the fourth was barely wide enough to accommodate the door that led into the passageway. The ceiling was covered with light-panels. There must have been a clothes closet in the compartment, but Sittas could not determine where it might be.

His inspection of the compact room took only a moment. As he shook hands with Vorgens and they both sat down facing each other, Sittas could see that the Watchman had changed.

It was nothing obvious, but Vorgens looked somehow different. He seemed well and hearty enough, but there were tiny lines around his eyes, and his face was slightly thinner, tauter. There was a different air about him. The Watchman was no longer a troubled, bewildered youth thrown into the middle of a world he could not understand. He was a Star Watch officer, in command of the Terran forces on this planet. He had accepted the responsibility of command, and had discovered at last that he could, to a degree, take that world into his own hands and begin to shape it for himself.

'I hear you were attacked on your way to join us,' Vorgens said, hunching forward slightly in the webbed chair.

Sittas shook his head. 'You could hardly call it an attack. Your troopers discovered a lone Komani warrior following our van. They fired a few beams at him, and he shot a small missile at us, which a trooper disposed of with another beam-gun. Then the Komani dropped out of range.'

'But he continued to follow you?'

'Yes. Until we reached the scoutcars at the perimeter of your encampment.'

Vorgens laughed. 'We're not camped here, Sittas, we're merely stopped for a few hours. I've been keeping the Mobile Force on the move constantly since we broke out of the valley.'

'Then it is true that you have assumed command.'

'I had to,' the Watchman answered, serious now. 'Aikens would not listen to reason. There was no one else to whom I could turn. I decided that I had more information about the situation than anyone else, so I took charge.'

'A Star Watch officer has such authority?'

'I do, now. Whether or not I had the right to take such authority into my own hands is a matter that will be settled by a Star Watch court, sometime in the future.'

Sittas leaned back in his webbed chair. 'The lieutenant you sent to Matara with the medical supplies said that you wanted to see me.'

'That's right,' Vorgens replied. 'First, I want to thank you again for your part in saving my life – and the lives of all the men in this Mobile Force. Nothing that we could do can ever repay the debt we all owe you.'

Sittas waved a hand of protest. 'That is all in the past. It is tomorrow that interests me – and you, I should judge.'

'Yes, tomorrow, and all the days that come after,' Vorgens agreed. He hesitated for a moment, framing the right words in his mind, then asked, 'If I invited the leaders of the Shinarian rebel movement to a truce conference here, would they come?'

The old priest shook his head. 'No, I doubt that they would.'

'Suppose I went to Capital City and asked them to meet with me there?'

'They would still smell a trap,' Sittas answered. 'They realize perfectly well that you do not know who they are. Why should they expose themselves?'

'I know Merdon.'

'Everyone on the planet knows Merdon. But he is only one of the leaders. He commands the youngest, and the most aggressive of the rebels, but there are many other groups – in the cities, in the hills, among the farming villages. They do not make up an army, as Merdon's people do, but they will fight in their own ways for Shinar's freedom. These are the people you must reach, and these are the leaders you do not know.'

'Then help me to meet them,' Vorgens pleaded earnestly. 'They trust you. Tell them that I want to discuss a peace settlement with them. Tell them that I'll meet them in Capital City, if they like, and they'll be guaranteed freedom from arrest.'

Sittas stroked his chin thoughtfully. 'They will still be revealing themselves to you. What's to stop you from having them arrested after the conference?'

'My word,' Vorgens replied, 'and your trust in me.'

'You are putting it up to me to bring the rebel leaders to your conference table,' the old man mused.

'You're the one man on this planet that both sides can trust.'

'That is very flattering.'

'And very true.'

Sittas shrugged. 'I suppose you have the right idea. We can lose nothing by trying.'

'Good!' Vorgens grinned broadly. 'You have the Mobile Force's communications equipment at your disposal.'

'Yes, using the tri-di would be faster than contacting each man in person. If they are not afraid to appear on tri-di and run the risk of having you Terrans trace their whereabouts.'

Vorgens shook his head. 'They have to take some risks. Peace isn't built on flowers and handshakes alone.'

It took four days to arrange the conference. Four days in which the Mobile Force, spread across the countryside like a moving cloud of giant insects, covered more than three hundred miles and fought six skirmishes with Komani attackers.

One of the clashes was fairly serious. A full battalion of Komani swooped down on a temporarily disabled light cruiser and two repair vans, just as dawn was breaking. The cruiser and her escorts were in the rear of the Terran formation, separated from the rest of the Mobile Force by a broad, swift-running river with thick woods on the far bank. The Komani reasoned that they could overwhelm the stragglers before any other Terran vehicles could get back to help.

The Komani warriors slashed across the sky with the sun at their backs and caught the surprised Terrans in the open. Before they could scramble into their vehicles, half the Terrans were killed or wounded, and one of the repair vans was in flames. The men aboard the cruiser quickly started to fight back, though, and frantically called for help.

The cruiser was being pounded by grenades, and the second repair van was badly damaged, when the Komani attackers were startled by movements in the woods across the river.

Trees seemed to be toppling, bursting into flame, exploding. As the turmoil approached the river bank, the Komani could see that a pair of battle cruisers was smashing through the woods, using their force beams to destroy the trees in front of them.

Finally the cruisers burst through the woods and started down the bank of the river. They did not pause a moment at the water, but skimmed right across, completely indifferent to the material underneath them.

As the Komani started to face the counterattack, another pair of Terran cruisers fell on them from the flank. The attackers were decimated; only a handful escaped the Terran envelopment.

Attacks on straggling vehicles ceased after that action.

The conference room that Sittas had picked was actually part of a church building. The room, warmly appointed in polished Shinarian wood, stood off to one side of the main chapel. It was a small chamber, with a central oblong table surrounded by leather-padded, high-backed chairs.

Vorgens sat at one side of the table, flanked by Sergeant McIntyre – whom the Watchman had made his personal aide – and Sittas. The priest introduced the eight Shinarians who sat across the table.

'And the spokesmen for all the groups represented at this meeting,' Sittas concluded, 'is Clanthas of Katan.'

Clanthas nodded pleasantly.

'You are Merdon's father?' Vorgens asked.

'Yes, I am.'

'I can see the family resemblance. The commander of the city garrison has told me quite a bit about you.'

Clanthas answered evenly, 'I could tell you quite a bit about the commander.'

'I imagine you could,' Vorgens said, grinning.

'We are ready to begin,' Clanthas said, 'if you are.'

'Is Merdon going to be here, or are you representing him?'

Clanthas' broad face clouded over. 'I do not know if Merdon intends to join this conference or not. No one here represents him, or his group.'

'I will represent Merdon.'

Vorgens turned round in his chair and saw Altai standing in the arched doorway of the conference room. She was still wearing a 'field uniform' of slacks and tunic, but somehow she looked more feminine than Vorgens had ever seen her to be.

The men rose from their seats. Altai went to the chair next to her uncle's and Sergeant McIntyre stepped over and held the chair as she sat down.

'I believe, then,' Vorgens said, 'that all the factions on Shinar are represented – with the exception of the Komani, who are not noticeably enthusiastic about truce conferences.'

They all murmured agreement.

'The purpose of this meeting is quite simple,' the Watchman began. 'Everyone here, I think, wants peace for Shinar. The question is: what is the cost of peace?'

'Merdon's price for peace is well known,' Altai said. 'He has instructed me to tell you that he will stop fighting when the Terrans leave Shinar. Freedom is his price.'

Vorgens nodded. 'And the official Terran price for peace is submission to the Empire. The Marines were sent to this planet to smash the rebellion and restore order under Terran terms.'

One of the Shinarians protested, 'Surely you cannot have called us here merely to tell us this!'

'Of course not,' Vorgens replied. 'I'm only trying to show that inflexibility on either side will only prolong the fighting.' Turning to Altai, he asked, 'Doesn't Merdon realize by now that if the Terrans should leave Shinar, your planet would become a prize for the Komani?'

Altai glanced at her uncle, then answered, 'Merdon believes that once the Terrans are driven off Shinar, Okatar Kang will want to attack the Empire somewhere else. He believes that we can be strong enough to prevent the Komani from overpowering us.'

'You know the rebel situation as well as Merdon does. Do you believe this too?'

'Merdon is our chief. He knows better than I.'

'But do you agree with him?' Vorgens asked.

After a long pause, she said, 'I'm only a girl. My opinion counts for very little.'

Clanthas broke into the conversation. 'Perhaps I should recapitulate the history of this rebellion. It started when the Empire began installing nutrient processing plants and uprooting our farmers. We appealed to the Terran governor, to no avail. We organized demonstrations, and the governor used troops to suppress us. Riots broke out. Many of the younger people – my son among them – decided to fight force with force. The governor was assassinated. The Marines were called in. The younger rebels asked the Komani to help us . . .'

'And here we are,' Sittas murmured.

'Exactly.' Clanthas said. 'The situation is completely out of control. All we want is for Shinar to be left in peace. We do not want to become a cog in your Empire. Neither do we want to become vassals of the Komani. Yet the Terrans and the Komani are fighting over us, turning our own world into a battleground. No matter who wins, we will lose.'

'All we want is to be left alone,' said another Shinarian.

Vorgens answered, quietly and patiently, 'That is a dream that will not come to pass in my lifetime or in yours. Shinar will not be left alone. It can't be left alone, no matter how much you wish it to be. If the Terrans don't make you part of their Empire, the Komani or someone else will. The simple truth is that Shinar is not powerful enough to remain completely independent. You never were. Before the Terrans, you were ruled by the Masters, remember. You were never alone. No nation is. Or could be.'

'Then what choice do we have?' a Shinarian blurted

miserably. 'Must we stand meekly by and watch you and the Komani rip our world to pieces in a battle to see which of you will be our overlord?'

'Your choice,' Vorgens reasoned, 'is one of degree. It may be possible, I think, for you to work out some system of self-government within the Terran Empire. I know that other nations have done this. I can't see why Shinar couldn't – in time. Within the Empire, there is the hope of eventual self-government. Not the total freedom that Merdon wants, perhaps, but a good part of it. Under the Komani, you have nothing to look forward to except destruction and death.'

Sittas countered. 'The Terrans have never permitted us the luxury of hoping for self-government before.'

'I know, and you have no official promise of it now, only my own feeling that, if we can act boldly and successfully in the next few weeks, the Empire might be more favorably disposed to hear your case.'

Clanthas' eyes narrowed. 'What are you suggesting?'

'Simply this. The Mobile Force can't defeat the Komani here on Shinar by itself. We can defend ourselves, and that's about all. Reinforcements are on their way, but Okatar Kang could ravage this planet quite thoroughly before they get here. If you want to prevent the Komani from destroying your world, you must help me to fight against them.

'Okatar has one weakness. He must win, here on Shinar. He must win quickly and decisively. If he can be held at bay, frustrated, kept off balance, then his dream of glory will soon fade. The other Komani clans will not ally themselves with him. Perhaps even his own people will become tired of fighting a fruitless war. Then, when the Star Watch reinforcements arrive, you, yourselves, will have achieved already a large part of the victory.

'The choice is yours to make. Either you fight for your own world, with the Terrans and against the Komani, or you allow the Komani to take over your planet, and you give them the springboard they want to touch off a galactic war.'

One of the Shinarians asked, 'Do you think that, if we help your troops fight the Komani, the Empire will look with favor on your request to govern ourselves?'

'I think they might, but I can't guarantee it.'

'You ask us to risk much for only the hope of freedom,' Clanthas said.

'Men have risked everything time and again,' Vorgens shot back, 'for the hope of freedom. It's the only hope you have.'

Altai laughed softly. 'What you're saying is that the threat of the Komani will force the Terrans to treat us with respect.'

'I am saying,' Vorgens answered firmly, 'that your own courage and self-respect are the only tools you have for achieving freedom. It's your choice. You must decide.'

'May I point out,' Sittas said, 'that we have here an official of the Terran Empire telling us to make our own decision about our own fate. That in itself is a milestone.'

The little group remained silent for a moment.

Finally Clanthas said, 'You are right, Watchman. It is a decision we must make for ourselves. Such a decision is not easily arrived at. We must have time to think. To discuss. You understand that?'

'Of course,' Vorgens said. 'But you must understand that time is precious, to all of us.'

Clanthas nodded. He rose from his chair, and everyone else got up.

'We will give you our answer within a few days.'

'Good enough,' Vorgens said.

More than an hour later, as their speedy little skimmer raced across the grassy countryside back to the main body of the Mobile Force, McIntyre said:

'I just hope that Star Watch Headquarters really does decide to send the reinforcements you told the natives we were gettin'.'

'So do I, Sergeant,' Vorgens answered fervently. 'So do I.'

CHAPTER FOURTEEN

POLES APART

The yellow sun of Shinar glittered brazenly on the sea and pressed its warmth into the long, curving, white beach. But the six young Shinarians trudging slowly along the sand paid no attention to the brilliant sun, nor to the steady, stiff breeze coming off the water, and the crashing surf that it propelled.

'And that's all that the Watchman had to say?' Merdon asked, rhetorically.

Altai nodded. 'It seemed to be a good beginning.'

'Beginning?' Merdon laughed. 'He's just asking us to go right back to where we started.'

'How did the other leaders take to his proposal?' Tarat asked.

'They seemed' – she hunted for the right word – 'impressed.'

'When you boil down to essentials,' Merdon said, 'the Watchman is asking us to help the Empire fight off the Komani. In return for this, he promises to do his best to get the Imperial bureaucracy to consider – consider, mind you – giving us some measure of freedom in the undetermined future.'

'What more can he do for us?' Altai asked.

'More? He hasn't done anything. Not a thing. The conference was a farce.'

'Well, maybe not,' Romal piped. 'The Watchman is giving us a chance to prove to the Terrans that we can take care of ourselves. After all, wouldn't the Empire be indebted to us if we helped to stop the Komani threat?'

Merdon glared down at his little quartermaster.

'What other choices do we have?' Altai insisted. 'The Komani haven't crushed the Mobile Force. The chances are that the war will go on for some time – until either the Terrans or the Komani bring enough reinforcements to Shinar to overpower the other. If we wait until that happens, we'll be at the mercy of the winner, whichever it may be.'

'Not if we help the Komani to smash the Terrans.'

Tarat objected, 'But the Empire is probably sending more troops here. We can't fight the whole Star Watch!'

'There are no reinforcements on their way here,' Merdon answered flatly. 'Okatar Kang is certain of that, and so am I.'

'How do you know?'

'He has his ways of finding out. Shinar is just a tiny pebble to the Terrans. They won't risk more men here until they realize that there's much more than our single planet involved. By the time they make up their minds, it'll be too late.'

'All this might have been true,' Altai said, 'if we had beaten the Mobile Force in the valley of Carmeer. But we haven't. The Mobile Force is still here, as strong as ever. The Watchman can fight the Komani indefinitely, if he has to.'

'Thanks to you.' Merdon snapped.

Altai stared at him, stunned.

'Well, you let him escape from the Komani. We had the Terrans boxed in, but he pulled them out of the trap. We had a chance to get rid of the Terrans, and you worked for them, instead of for us.'

For several moments, no one spoke.

Finally Altai replied, in a voice trembling with pain and anger, 'If I hadn't helped the Watchman, if we had fought the battle that you were hoping to fight, most of us would be dead right now, and Okatar would be ruling this planet.'

'Shinar would be free, you mean.'

'No, Merdon, you're wrong. If we must choose between the Terrans and the Komani, I will go with the Terrans.'

'What about freedom for Shinar?'

'There are more ways to obtain freedom than with a gun,' she said.

Merdon looked at the four youths, watching them waiting for his next reaction.

'All right, then,' he said, with a deadly calm, 'you can go with the Terrans if you like. I won't stop you.'

Without another word, Altai turned her back on Merdon and walked away. In shocked silence, the others watched her stride up the beach, toward the groundcars parked on the grassy dunes above.

'If any of the rest of you feel the same way, now's the time to say it.'

The four young lieutenants glanced uneasily at each other. Ron shuffled his weight from one foot to the other, then blurted out, 'I'm sorry, Merdon. She's right and you're not. I'm going with her.'

He broke into a run, following Altai's footsteps.

Tarat shook his head. 'There'll be others joining them when they hear about this.'

'Let them go,' growled Merdon, furious, 'They'll crawl back to us when we've freed Shinar.'

Altai climbed up the dune and reached the groundcar without noticing Ron following her. She opened the door of the little bubble-topped car and dropped into the driver's seat. Only then did she allow herself to break into the tears that she had been holding back.

Okatar Kang paced his tent like a caged jungle beast, while his council of nobles sat passively at their long table and watched their chieftain.

'So the Terrans have been talking with the native leaders, have they? These spineless Shinarians blow with the wind. When we had the Terrans trapped, they were pleased with us. Now that there is more fighting to be done, they're not so sure.'

'The natives are no immediate threat to us, Lord Okatar,' said one of the nobles. 'It is the Terrans.'

'The Terrans!' Okatar spat. 'They're lucky to be alive, and they know it. They are merely trying to protect themselves; they are no danger.'

'But still, they have a powerful force.'

'I wish they would offer us battle,' Okatar said. 'We would overwhelm them, once and for all. But, no, instead they retreat, they flee from us. Very well. Let them run.'

'What have you in mind?'

Okatar stopped his pacing and faced the council table. 'We are going to make this planet feel the full might of the Komani. Until now we have attempted to deal with the Shinarians as allies. But they have betrayed us. Now we shall treat them as subjects. This planet is ours for the taking, and I intend to take what we want from it.'

'What about the Shinarian forces still allied to us?'

'They have plotted against us. Merdon and his children's army have hoped that we would drive off the Terrans, and then be so weakened that they could drive us off.'

'Do you intend to force Merdon to join the Terrans?'

'That, he will never do. No, I intend to offer him a bargain – a bargain on Komani terms. He can still serve with us, but as a subject, not an ally. When we are finished with Shinar, he can take control of the planet, but he will be our subject.'

'If he refuses this bargain?'

'He will die.'

'And the Terrans?'

Okatar smiled fiercely, 'We shall start a campaign of terror and looting that will turn this planet upside-down. We shall take what we need and what we want from the Shinarian countryside and the towns that have no Terran garrison. Sooner or later, the Terrans will be forced to offer us battle. They will stop running and try to attack our forces; possibly they will attempt to attack this camp. When they mass, we will mass. When they attempt to strike at us, we will destroy them!'

'In the meantime, we will be gathering supplies and equipment from the natives.'

'Exactly so,' Okatar said. 'With every day, our strength will grow, and the Shinarians' dread of our power will grow equally. With every day, the Terrans will become weaker.'

As the exec sat in Vorgens' quarters and listened to what the Star Watchman was telling him, his eyes widened more and more, until white showed almost all the way around them.

'I – I can't believe you mean what you're saying,' the exec protested.

Sergeant McIntyre, standing at the doorway to the tiny cubicle, nodded grimly. 'Neither could I, when he told me, sir. Can't you talk him outta doin' it?'

Vorgens half turned in his webbed chair and surveyed the Sergeant with a wry smile. 'My aide, here,' he said to the exec, 'said he thinks the idea is crazy.'

'It's certainly . . . unusual,' the exec said, lamely.

The smile faded from Vorgens' face. 'Unusual or not, do you think the idea is sound?'

'From a military point of view, yes sir, I do,' the exec admitted, nodding. 'But from your own personal point—'

'That's *my* problem,' Vorgens said, abruptly getting up from the webbed chair. 'All right, if it's sound militarily, we've got to do it. Let's go.'

'Now?' McIntyre asked.

'Right now, and I want the two of you along as witnesses.'

With a frown on his beefy face, McIntyre led the way down the narrow passage to Brigadier Aikens' quarters. When the sergeant hesitated at the door, Vorgens knocked.

'Come.'

McIntyre opened the door, and the three of them stepped in. Aikens was lying in his bunk, reading a report projected overhead.

The brigadier cocked an eye at Vorgens, then swung up to a sitting position. The projector automatically shut off.

'To what do I owe this honor?'

'Was that the Officer of the Day's report you were scanning?' Vorgens asked.

'That's right. I like to keep up on what you're doing with my men. Any objections?'

'No. None at all . . . May we come in?'

Aikens gestured to the unfolded writing desk and the pair of webbed chairs flanking it. 'Make yourself at home. You're in command, aren't you?'

McIntyre could see Vorgens' whole body stiffen at the brigadier's sarcasm. The Watchman took one of the chairs. The exec and the sergeant remained standing.

'I trust you've been physically comfortable,' Vorgens said.

'Don't play games with me, Watchman. You're up to something. Now what is it?'

'You've been keeping track of the Mobile Force's actions.' It was a statement, not a question.

'Yes, of course.'

'Good. I've been thinking over the situation for the past two days, and I've come to a decision . . .'

'And you expect me to give you advice? Don't waste your time.'

Vorgens clenched his fists. For a moment, he said nothing. Then, with a visible effort to remain calm, he resumed, 'I'm not looking for advice, but I do have a question to ask you. Your answer will affect the lives of the men of this Mobile Force, and the lives of every man, woman and child on Shinar.'

For the first time, Aikens looked directly at the Watchman. 'Well?'

'I want to know if you're willing to resume command of the Mobile Force.'

Aikens' eyes flashed for an instant. Then he asked slowly, 'Resume command? What brought you to that decision? You made it pretty clear that I'm unfit to command.'

'Brigadier, don't make this any harder than it has to be. I assumed command because I represent the authority of Star Watch Headquarters, and you were unwilling to follow the policies expressed by my orders.'

Aikens glared at the Watchman, but said nothing.

'It's quite obvious,' Vorgens went on, 'that my training as a Star Watch officer can never match your experience as a commander in the field. I took over the command of this Force because it was the only way to get us out of the Komani trap. But I have no delusions about my ability to direct a full-scale planetary action. The situation calls for an able, experienced field commander. Are you willing to resume command, or not?'

The brigadier grinned humorlessly. 'I knew you'd be handing the ball back to me sooner or later. You haven't got the backbone for this kind of responsibility.'

Strangely, Vorgens smiled back at the older man. 'Perhaps you don't understand me,' he said. 'I want you to resume command of the Mobile Force . . . *under my authority*. I am in charge of all Terran forces on Shinar, and until a higher-ranking Watchman reaches the planet, I shall remain in command. I'm offering you tactical control of the Mobile Force; strategic decisions will be made by me.'

'You . . . you . . .' Aikens' face glowered red, and the rage seemed to well up in his throat, choking him. 'You're offering me – tactical command – under your authority! I – I'll . . .'

'Before you say anything else,' Vorgens warned, his voice

suddenly as sharp as a cutting beam, 'I'll be forced to turn over the job to the executive officer, if you don't accept the command.'

Aikens half rose off the edge of the bunk, then sat down again. His face turned a mottled purplish color.

'I'm sorry that it has to be this way,' Vorgens said, more gently, 'but I can't see any other way.'

'All right, Watchman,' Aikens said, after several moments' silence, 'I'll resume command of the Mobile Force. I'll pull your little carcass out of the fire . . . and when we've settled this business on Shinar, I'll call for a court-martial so fast your head will swim.'

Vorgens nodded. 'I'm sure a court of inquiry will be necessary to straighten out our differences. But, for the moment, let's hope we can both rise above our personal feelings.'

'I'm a soldier, youngster; I know how to keep my feelings to myself when it's for the good of the men. But don't have any illusions. We're poles apart, you and me. Now and always. Understand?'

'Perfectly.'

Vorgens walked back to the dreadnaught's control center in silence. His face was immobile. He felt empty and drained of emotion.

It was a complete surprise to see Altai sitting at an untended control desk. The trooper on watch said to Vorgens:

'She just showed up at one of the scoutcars on the perimeter and said she wanted to see you, sir. Wouldn't talk to anyone else.'

The Watchman went to her. Altai's face was outwardly calm, but Vorgens could sense the tenseness within her. Her dark eyes showed no trace of the tears she had been shedding.

'You wanted to see me?' he asked, sitting down next to her.

'I've left Merdon,' she said quietly. 'Several squads of our fighters have decided to join you and fight against the Komani. They are waiting for your orders.'

'I see. And Merdon?'

'He . . .' For just an instant it seemed her self-control

would crack. 'He refuses to change his mind. He will fight against you, he says, until Shinar is free.'

'I'm sorry to hear that,' Vorgens replied, 'and sorrier still to see you so – upset. He means very much to you, doesn't he?'

'Once he did,' she said. 'Now, we couldn't be farther apart if we were on opposite ends of the world.'

Vorgens smiled at her.

'What's so funny?'

'It's not funny, merely an odd coincidence. Someone just told me that I was poles apart from him.'

'You? You're among your own men, why should you worry about one person?'

'He's a very important person. And as far as being among my own men . . . I'm among strangers. With the exception of two or three people, I've known you and your uncle longer than any of the men here.'

'You're as alone as I am,' Altai said.

'Yes,' Vorgens agreed. 'That's right.'

CHAPTER FIFTEEN

CHOICES AND PLANS

The Komani warrior sat under a tree at the crest of a hill overlooking Shinar's Capital City. He had lost track of the days since he had first started hunting the old priest, first at the town of Matara, then along the road to the Mobile Force's camp, and finally here at the city.

He could not follow his prey into the city, of course. The Terran garrison would shoot him on sight. So he waited, living off terrified farmers and villagers nearby, sleeping in the open, waiting with remorseless patience. Sooner or later, the priest would leave the city, and he could be attacked or killed.

As he sat with his broad back against the sturdy shade tree, the warrior studied the city spread out on the plain below. It was the biggest collection of buildings he had ever seen, even larger than the rare clan gatherings of the Komani, which covered whole valleys with bubble-tents.

A thought drifted across his mind like a dark cloud: What if the priest left the city by a road other than the one he came in on? There were many roads into and out of the city. What if the priest was no longer there, and had escaped?

The warrior pondered over the matter. The priest did not know he was being stalked. There was no reason for him to leave the city stealthily. On the other hand, there was no reason for him to choose the road the Komani was watching.

After a long struggle with the problem, the warrior finally made a decision. He would return to Matara. If the priest left the city, he was bound to turn up at the hospital again, sooner or later. Time was of no importance. And, besides, at Matara there were many other Komani available for companionship.

The warrior rose, took a last look at Capital City, and turned toward Matara.

Vorgens sat at the command desk in the deserted control center and sifted through the morning's reports. The Komani were stepping up their activities; strikes against the perimeter of the Mobile Force, raids against isolated villages and farms, even a hit-and-run attack on one of the larger cities. They were spreading terror and destruction all around Shinar.

As he read through the reports, Vorgens' mind kept turning over other problems. Aikens had not come out of his quarters since their conversation, three days ago. If the brigadier was willing to take tactical command of the Mobile Force, he had yet to show it. The rebels still had not contacted him, even though more than a week had gone by since their conference in Capital City.

Altai stepped through one of the hatches and entered the control center.

'Are you busy?' she asked.

'Not terribly. Have your people found adequate quarters?'

She nodded as she made her way through the compact maze of desks and consoles and sat down beside the Watchman. 'Yes, there's an old monastery nearby. Once the monks learned that Sittas is my uncle, they allowed us to stay. The boys sleep in the cellar, the girls in the barn.'

Vorgens grinned. 'Sounds charming. But, you know, we won't be in this area much longer. Do you intend to follow us, or stay here?'

'I think we'll stay here for the time being – until we decide on what to do.'

'We've all got some decisions to make, and not much more time to waste before we make them. The Komani are beginning to run wild all over the planet.'

'I know,' she said. 'Have you received any further word from Star Watch Headquarters about reinforcements?'

'Nothing definite,' Vorgens admitted. 'Reinforcements are being prepared, but I can't get firm word on how much and how soon.'

The desktop viewscreen at his elbow chimed softly. Vorgens touched the control stud.

'Message for you, sir. From Capital City.'

'Is it the garrison commander?'

'Relayed through his office, sir. But the message is from a native. Clanthas . . .'

'Put him through!'

Vorgens glanced at Altai as the viewscreen began to glow with color. She looked as excited as he felt.

Clanthas' broad, slightly jowly face filled the screen. 'A good day to you, Watchman. And to you, Altai.'

'And the same to you,' Vorgens replied. 'I've been waiting for your call.'

The merchant assumed a slightly apologetic expression. 'It took somewhat longer than I expected, but I think you'll find my news worth the waiting.' He paused dramatically. 'The other leaders and I have decided to take you at your word. We will help you and work against the Komani in whatever way possible.'

Only now did Vorgens realize he had been holding his breath. He exhaled slowly and murmured, 'You did it.'

'Don't overestimate my powers of persuasion,' Clanthas said. 'Most of the leaders were dead set against working with the Empire. Even now the best that can be said is that they are going ahead with grave misgivings, but with the Komani killing and looting everywhere . . . we really have no choice.'

'Except surrendering to the Komani.'

'We discussed that possibility,' Clanthas admitted cheerfully, 'and rejected it. We will help you – or allow you to help us, depending on how you look at the matter.'

'We will work together to defeat the Komani and bring peace to Shinar,' Vorgens said, firmly.

'And then what?' Altai asked.

Vorgens turned to her. 'Then we will work together just as hard to give your people the freedom for which they are fighting.'

'Amen to that,' Clanthas said. 'Well . . . now that we're at your disposal, what are your plans for us? Most of my people are not organized into fighting groups, the way Merdon's units are. But they can help to defend themselves, if you'll show them what to do, and give them some weapons.'

Vorgens nodded. 'Our plans haven't crystallized yet. But your decision should certainly clarify our thinking. I'll call you back as soon as we have drawn up a comprehensive picture. Will you remain in Capital City?'

136

'I think not,' Clanthas said. 'I'm going back to Katan.'

'Is my uncle still with you?'

'He was, until this morning. Helped tremendously in convincing the other leaders that you were trustworthy, too. He started back to the hospital at Matara this morning. Should be there by nightfall.'

The three of them chatted for a few minutes longer. When Clanthas' image had faded from the viewscreen, Vorgens touched a button and called for McIntyre.

The Sergeant's face took form on the screen.

'Please give my compliments to Brigadier Aikens and ask him to meet me in the control center as soon as possible. Tell him that the native leaders have decided to work with us, and we must draw up a battle plan immediately.'

'Yes sir,' said the sergeant.

Within a half an hour, Aikens, the executive officer, and the top officers of the Mobile Force's staff were crowding the control center. Vorgens was still at the command desk, with Altai beside him and McIntyre standing behind.

'I have already drawn up two tactical plans,' Aikens said, with a slightly malicious emphasis on the word *tactical*. He dropped two thick notebooks on Vorgens' desk.

'One of the plans is based on the assumption that the natives will not aid us, and I assume that such an assumption is now outdated.'

'That's right,' Vorgens said.

'Very well then.' Aikens tapped on the cover of one of the notebooks. 'This is the plan to use, in that case.'

Vorgens opened the book and thumbed through it. 'Very detailed,' he said. Then looking up at the brigadier, he asked. 'Would you care to give me a brief rundown on the main features of the plan?'

'It's quite simple,' the brigadier said. 'Have you ever seen what happens when you put a drop of ink into a glass of clear water?'

Vorgens' eyebrows arched, and his forehead wrinkled. 'Why . . . the color spreads through the whole glass.'

'Exactly. Now suppose that the glass of water is a certain district of this planet, open to attack by the Komani. And the drop of ink—'

'The drop of ink would be a unit of Marines,' Vorgens said.

137

'Very good, Watchman! You're quite astute today.'

Vorgens' eyes flashed angrily for a moment, then he regained his self-control and answered, 'I have my moments. Evidently what you're proposing to do is to split up the Mobile Force into small units and spread them through Shinar.'

'Right,' Aikens said. 'Each unit will be strong enough to fend off a Komani raiding party, and the units will be spaced close enough together so that one group could come to the aid of another, in case the Komani mount an unusually heavy attack.'

'And what if the Komani mass a really large force, such as they did in Carmeer?'

It was Aikens' turn to flush with anger. For a moment he said nothing. Then, finally, 'We will depend to some extent on the natives for intelligence reports. If we learn that the Komani are massing for a full-scale battle, we will also mass our forces.'

'Fine,' Vorgens said. 'Now, how much territory can we protect in this manner?'

Aikens took up the notebook from Vorgens' desk and riffled to a page toward the back. 'We analyzed the cruising speed of our vehicles, the logistics problem, our response time to an attack-alert, and other factors . . . the computer came up with an answer.' He showed the page of computations to the Watchman. 'We can cover roughly half the populated area of the planet.'

'And the other half?'

Aikens shrugged his shoulders.

'Have you assumed that the natives would be armed?'

'No.'

'Suppose we armed them and trained them . . . couldn't we gradually extend our protection to the whole planet, then?'

Aikens hesitated a moment, then, looking at Altai, he answered, 'We could arm the natives and train them briefly. But could we trust them?'

Vorgens replied instantly, 'They're trusting us, brigadier. So I guess we'll have to trust them.'

'I see.'

'It's a good plan,' Vorgens said. 'Please take the necessary steps to put it into operation immediately, and contact the garrison commanders at the four cities we now hold. Tell them that you'll be taking some of the stocks from their arsenals to give to the natives.'

Aikens glowered. 'I will do so only under protest.'

'Do it anyway you like,' Vorgens said. 'But do it.'

After Aikens and his staff had cleared out of the control center, Altai said, 'I would like to go to Matara briefly and see my uncle once more. It looks as though we'll be fighting again soon, and I'd like to visit him while I can.'

'All right,' Vorgens said. 'I'd like to see him, too. Sergeant, how long would it take us to drive over to Matara?'

McIntyre thought for a moment. 'I could get you there on a scrambler before nightfall.'

The farmer's truck was ancient and slow. Sittas, already bone-weary from a solid week of pleading and cajoling with the rebel leaders at Capital City, was even too tired to pay attention to the flaming colors of the sky as Oran dipped behind the hills that surrounded Matara. Soon they would be back at the hospital, and he could rest. The farmer, sitting in the driver's seat, was too awed by his unexpected guest to utter a word throughout the long, hot, dusty trip.

It was dusk when the truck finally pulled into the town square of Matara. The normally placid air of the place was still banished by the bustle of activity connected with the hospital. A Komani litter, buoyed by four of the versatile one-man flyers, hovered at the bottom of the town hall's steps. Evidently more wounded warriors had just arrived. Merchants and farmers had set up stalls along one side of the square, to supply the makeshift hospital with the goods (and a few luxuries) that it required. People of all descriptions were coming and going through the square. Even a Terran scrambler was parked in front of the hospital, Sittas noticed.

He climbed down stiffly from the truck and started toward the steps that led into the town-hall-turned-hospital.

Altai appeared at the door, atop the steps, and ran down to meet him.

'So here you are!' she said. 'Clanthas told us you were coming here. We got here before you.'

'We?' the old man asked, slightly puzzled.

139

'The Watchman and his aide and I. We came to see you. Vorgens and the sergeant are inside. He's amazed with the hospital.'

'I see . . .'

A Komani warrior, dusty and travel-stained, advanced on them. 'You are the one called Sittas?'

The old man turned to face the Komani. 'Yes, I am Sittas.'

The warrior drew his ceremonial sword. 'In the of name Lord Okatar, I must take your life.'

Everyone froze. The square, pulsating with life an instant earlier, became as still as death. No one moved, even the breeze seemed to die, as the Komani held his sword before him, pointed directly at the old priest.

It was Altai who broke the spell. She stepped in front of Sittas and said, 'You cannot kill him!'

'You are a woman, and unarmed. Stand aside.'

'You'll have to kill me first.'

Before the warrior could reply, the farmer who had driven the truck rushed up and stood beside the girl. 'And me too!'

Immediately, everyone in the square began to throng around the warrior. There was not a weapon on any of them, but they stood there, unmoving, as the Komani watched them through his unblinking, yellow cat's eyes.

With his free hand, the warrior reached for the pistol on his belt. Before he could grasp it, a beam lanced through his shoulder. The warrior sagged to the ground. His sword clattered on the paving stones.

Everyone turned, and saw Vorgens and McIntyre at the top of the town hall steps. The sergeant held a gun in his massive fist.

Vorgens dashed down the steps, with McIntyre at his heels. The crowd opened a lane for them.

'He was going to kill us!' Altai sobbed.

Vorgens put his arm around her. 'It's all right. It's all right.'

The warrior painfully climbed to his knees and began to reach for the sword that he had dropped.

McIntyre stamped a heavy boot on the sword and put his gun to the Komani's head.

'Don't kill him!' Sittas cried. 'He was only following the orders of Okatar.'

Without taking his eyes from the warrior, McIntyre said, 'I know how they think. As long as this one lives, he'll have nothin' else on his mind but killin' you.'

'Does that mean that I must have him killed?' Sittas asked.

'Take the gun away from him and place him under guard,' Vorgens ordered.

'It is fortunate that you came when you did,' Sittas said to the Watchman.

Vorgens looked around at the crowd. 'It looks to me as though you had quite a bit of help without us.'

It was late at night when Vorgens and McIntyre returned to the Mobile Force. Most of the dreadnaught's crewmen were asleep. Altai had stayed at Matara, and the Komani warrior had been placed under Shinarian custody.

A yellow light flashing at the command desk told Vorgens that a message was waiting for him. He activated the viewscreen and scanned the words printed on it.

'Is it from Star Watch Headquarters?' McIntyre asked eagerly.

Vorgens slumped into his seat. 'Yes, it is.'

McIntyre stepped over beside the Watchman to read the screen:

MINIMAL RELIEF FLEET OF THREE STARSHIPS AND NORMAL COMPLEMENT OF MARINES WILL ARRIVE AT SHINAR, IN SIX WEEKS. SWHQ.

'Three ships,' McIntyre said, stunned. 'Three lousy ships.'

'A token force,' Vorgens said. 'I suppose that they feel we're not worth risking more men and ships.'

'But that ain't gonna do us any good at all!'

'I know. It will prove what Okatar's been saying all along – that the Empire isn't able to meet the strength of the combined Komani clans. It would've been better if they had decided not to send any reinforcements at all.'

CHAPTER SIXTEEN

'SHINAR HAS BEEN CONQUERED'

Merdon gnawed fretfully on his lower lip as he sat before the blank viewscreen. Standing outside the tri-di booth were Tarat and Romal. The trio were in the abandoned nutrient-processing plant where Merdon had hidden a cache of weapons.

'Is he going to speak to you or not?' Romal asked nervously.

'He'll come on,' Merdon said. 'He'd better.'

As if in answer to the young rebel leader, the viewscreen seemed to dissolve and the powerful form of Okatar took shape. The Komani Kang was seated in his tent. Although no one else was in the line-of-view, Merdon sensed that Okatar was far from alone.

'I have asked you to come to my camp,' Okatar said. 'Why do you refuse, and attempt to speak through the tri-di? It is difficult to confer fully with you in this manner.'

Merdon sat without answering for a moment, and the two stared at each other, face to face. Finally Merdon said, 'Shall I be frank?'

'By all means.'

'I was going to visit your camp, but my lieutenants asked me not to, for two reasons. First, they feel that you have broken the bonds of friendship and common purpose that we once had between us. Second, they fear that I might never leave your camp – alive.'

'You have suspicious friends,' Okatar said impassively.

'They value my life more than I do, perhaps. But I agree with them on the first point – your raids on our people are not the works of an ally.'

Okatar nodded. 'Correct. I have learned that your people are no longer allies of the Komani. They were friendly with us only when it seemed that the Terrans would be wiped out in the valley of Carmeer. Now that there is the prospect of continued fighting before us, your people have meekly returned to the Terrans and asked to be forgiven for their audacious dreams of freedom.'

'And because they are weak you attack them,' Merdon snapped.

'The Komani take what they want. If your people resist, we use force. The time for wheedling and coaxing is past. If we fail on Shinar, everything fails, and I will not see the Komani conquest of the Terran Empire thwarted by a herd of self-pitying sheep!'

'We can fight!' Merdon shouted. 'We've shown that we can. We've stood up to the Terrans before. It's *you* who has driven my people back into the arms of the Terrans.'

Okatar raised a massive hand. 'The time for discussion and argument is past. To all intents and purposes, Shinar has been conquered. The Terrans are content to huddle within their cities or inside the armored vehicles of their Mobile Force. These raids on your people have shown that the Terrans will not fight for Shinarians, but only to save themselves. Shinar is ours. Those who resist us will be crushed.'

'And you'll take what you want from us,' Merdon said dully.

'Exactly so.'

'Suppose . . . suppose you drew up a list of the supplies and equipment you need. Suppose I could convince my people to give you what you require. Would you leave Shinar in peace then?'

The faintest hint of a smile flickered across Okatar's face. 'If such a bargain could be arranged, I would consider striking at the next Terran target.'

'And leave Shinar?'

'Yes, I would leave Shinar . . . Of course, one of my nobles would remain behind as governor of this planet. He would see to it that you continued to honor my requirements for supplies.'

'And the Terrans?'

'The Terrans on Shinar would be forced to withdraw when I struck the next planet, or else their lines of supply with the rest of the Empire would be cut.'

Merdon nodded. 'Yes, and Shinar would be free of them.'

'Shinar would be a vassal of the Komani,' Okatar said.

'In return for our protection, we would expect tribute.'

'Tribute,' Merdon echoed, 'and the first payment would be the list of supplies and equipment you'd need to attack the next Terran planet.'

'Correct,' said Okatar.

Merdon glanced at his two lieutenants, outside the tri-di booth. They both seemed to be in an agony of impatience.

'I must discuss this with my people,' Merdon told Okatar. 'I will call you again, shortly.'

'Very well,' Okatar replied. The viewscreen went blank.

As Merdon stepped out of the booth, Romal yelped, 'Do you realize what you're saying? Okatar will demand everything his men can carry . . . he'll strip us bare!'

'You can't be serious about this,' Tarat added. 'We can't ask our people to give the Komani whatever they want.'

Merdon folded his arms across his chest and stared them both into silence. 'I don't see that we have any choice in the matter,' he said firmly.

Clanthas basked in the warm sunshine flooding the broad veranda that surrounded the upper floor of his house in Katan. Beyond the railing of the veranda, the flat white roofs of other houses marched down the sloping hillside to the bright blue waters of the harbor. Across the harbor was the busy port of Katan, where the farm produce from a thousand miles around was gathered together and loaded on the big sea-going transports which skimmed across Shinar's oceans and lands with equal ease.

Seemingly sitting across the veranda from the merchant was the tri-di image of Vorgens. The Star Watchman had been explaining, for the past half-hour, the Terran plan of action which Brigadier Aikens had drawn up.

'Let me see if I understand this correctly,' Clanthas said. 'The Marines will set up small task units – based on your armored vehicles – in the villages, towns, and cities. They will give arms to the people and teach them how to fight. They will patrol the farmlands until the people themselves are able to guard their own land. Then they will move on to another district and repeat the same procedure.'

Vorgens nodded. 'That's right. The ultimate goal is to have the entire planet covered by either Terran Marines or your own people. We want to deny the use of your land to the Komani – to fence them in, so to speak.'

'Suppose the Komani mass for a major attack?' Clanthas asked. 'They still outnumber your Mobile Force by a great margin.'

'If they mass, we'll have to face them. I hope that we'll have enough time to train a good number of your people, and that they will be fighting alongside us, in the event of a major battle.'

Clanthas murmured agreement.

'What we're trying to do,' Vorgens went on, 'is to throttle down the Komani raids on your people. We're trying to keep the skirmishes and fighting down as much as possible.'

'I understand. Still, it appears that there is no end to the fighting in sight.'

'True enough,' Vorgens admitted.

Clanthas suddenly shifted the subject. 'Do you know why this rebellion began? I mean, the real reason?'

'I think I do,' Vorgens said, 'but I'd like to hear your opinion.'

'The reason goes back more than a century, to the time when we were still dominated by the Masters. You see, the Masters saw to it that we remained a static nation. Our population was fixed at about 500 million, and we never rose much above that figure.'

'Yes, I know,' Vorgens said.

'In those days,' Clanthas went on, 'Shinar fed not only itself, but all the worlds within fifteen lightyears of our planet. We were not prosperous, of course, but we were in equilibrium with the rest of the Masters' domain. We knew what to expect, from one day to the next.'

'And then the Terrans came.'

'Yes. The Terrans crushed the Masters and liberated Shinar. We were suddenly thrown on our own devices. For a while, everything continued as it had always gone. But something important had changed. Slowly, at first, and then with explosive speed, our population began to grow. When I was Merdon's age, Shinar had two billion people; now we have three billion.'

'And it is difficult for you to feed yourselves,' Vorgens said.

'Not yet difficult, but that day is fast approaching. However, we must use all the food we produce to feed ourselves. Practically nothing is left for export. Our trade with the other worlds around us is dying, and we are becoming a bankrupt nation. *That* is the underlying reason behind the people's resentment of the Empire. The installation of the food processing plants was merely the trigger. They already hated the Terrans, because they were becoming overcrowded and pauperized, under the Empire.'

'But couldn't they see that the nutrient plants were the answer to their problem?' Vorgens asked. 'Didn't the governor explain that the processing plants would enable you to multiply your output of foodstuffs many times over, and reopen your trade with the other planets?'

Clanthas shrugged. 'A proclamation of that sort was issued, but very little effort was made to explain things to the farmers. All they knew was that they were being moved off their farms to make room for the Terran factories.'

Vorgens shook his head. 'I was afraid that this was the case. Evidently the Terran governor didn't realize that people can't change their whole way of living overnight – even when it's extremely necessary for them to do so.'

'It may be necessary,' Clanthas answered, 'but hardly desirable.'

'I realize that, but the planets that depended on your food a few decades ago are now going hungry, to a large extent. From the Empire's point of view, the problem of Shinar affects all of Shinar's neighbors. If we can't solve your problem, and solve it soon, rebellion against the Empire might well break out elsewhere. That's what I fear most,' Vorgens said worriedly, 'that this movement against the Empire will spread to other planets. If it does – or if the Komani decide to attack another Empire planet – then there'll be no way to stop a general war from developing. We've got to keep this problem confined to Shinar, and solve it here. Otherwise we've lost.'

The argument had raged hotly while Merdon, Tarat, and Romal paced the length and breadth of the idle nutrient-processing plant.

'You're going to ask our people to strip their homes, their

146

farms, their cities, and give everything to the Komani. They won't do it!' Tarat bellowed.

'They'll have to,' Merdon said evenly. 'The Komani will just take it anyway.'

'No, no, no,' Romal said, his round face flushed with agitation. 'The people are willing to fight the Komani.'

Merdon laughed bitterly. 'Then the Komani will take what they want and kill our people, too.'

Tarat shook his head. 'I never thought I'd see you give up.'

Anger flashed in Merdon's eyes. Then he replied quietly, 'Can we beat the Komani?'

'No, but . . .'

'Do we want them off Shinar?'

'Of course.'

'Will their attack on another planet force the Terrans to leave Shinar?'

'Probably it will,' Tarat admitted.

'Then I don't see that we have any choice,' Merdon said. 'I don't like it any more than you do, but if it will get rid of both the Terrans and the Komani . . .'

'How do you know it'll work out that way?' Tarat said. 'There's only one chance in a million.'

'Then I'll take that one chance!' Merdon snapped.

'But it's so dangerous, Merdon,' Romal pleaded. 'Maybe the best thing to do, after all, would be to put in with the Terrans. At least they're not as bad as the Komani, and the Watchman said . . .'

'It would be safer to join the Terrans,' Merdon said softly. Then, his voice rising, he continued, 'It would have been safer still never to have tried to rebel against them, but we weren't interested in safety then. We wanted freedom! Now that things look black, are we going to turn our backs on our hopes, our dreams? Are we going to tell our people: "Go on back home, the whole thing was a big mistake? Go home and ask the Terrans to forgive you"? Well, are we?'

'What else can we do, Merdon?' Tarat asked. 'Let the Komani rule us in the Terrans' place?'

'No! I'll tell you what we can do. We can dare! We can take that one chance in a million and make it work for us – or die trying. As long as there is that one chance – no matter

147

how slim it might be – we've got to risk everything for it. Do you understand? *We've got to.* Otherwise everything we've done so far is wasted. The men who've died for our cause, died for nothing. The people who believe that we will fight to the last drop of sweat and blood to make Shinar free, will have been hoodwinked.

'I know how hard it will be to fill the Komani's demands. I'm not sure that we can convince the people to make this sacrifice, even for their own eventual freedom, but I'm going to try! Who will follow me?'

Tarat scratched nervously at his cheek, glanced at little Romal, and then said softly, 'Well, if you think there's really a chance that we can get rid of both the Terrans and the Komani . . .'

'We won't be rid of the Komani,' Romal argued. 'You heard what Okatar said. There'll be a Komani governor over us.'

'We had a Terran governor over us once. Where is he now?'

Romal blinked. 'He's – he was – assassinated.'

'And what's to stop us from driving off a Komani governor, after the warriors have left Shinar? What would the Komani governor have to back up his word, except our own fear of Okatar?'

'That would be enough,' Tarat said. 'If we didn't behave, Okatar could have the whole Komani nation on our backs in no time flat.'

'Not if they're fighting the whole Terran Empire. Shinar could still become free while the Terrans and the Komani exhaust themselves in their war.'

Romal shook his head. 'That's an awfully long gamble to take.'

'But if it works . . .'

'Fine, if it works,' Tarat said. 'But what if it doesn't?'

'It'll work,' Merdon said stubbornly. 'It's *got* to.'

Within a few minutes, the Shinarian youth sat facing Okatar on the viewscreen while his lieutenants stood uneasily off to one side.

'Draw up your list,' Merdon said firmly, 'and I'll try to get my people to meet your needs. But the list must be kept to essentials. We don't intend to supply tribute. Shinar is a poor planet. There'll be plenty of booty for you elsewhere in the Empire.'

'True enough,' Okatar said, noncommittally. 'I will instruct my seneschal to prepare the list.'

'Very well.'

'Oh yes, there is one other item which I want to make clear to you,' Okatar said. 'I have sent a column of warriors to investigate rumors about a well-stocked arsenal, and warehouses filled with food, in the city of Katan. I intend that they should carry through this investigation, even if they must use force. I don't want to have the feeling that anyone – including you – might be hiding things from me.'

Abruptly, the viewscreen went blank.

CHAPTER SEVENTEEN

MERDON

Vorgens perched atop the cab of a troop carrier and watched the Marines working with the farmers under the bright, hot sun of Shinar. The meadow spread out before him was dotted with groups of men and machines. The Terrans, in their bright uniforms, helmets and glare visors towered impressively over the indifferently dressed, dark-skinned little farmers.

One knot of men was clustered around a dismantled heavy beamgun. The Shinarians were learning how to put it back together. Another group was tinkering with field communications helmets. Close by the troop carrier, a young captain was lecturing the village elders on modern theories of defense in depth against flying Komani attacks. Farther off, near the edge of the meadow, a platoon of youngsters was peppering a grove of trees with small arms fire.

This had been the first day, the first experiment in the joint Terran-Shinarian defense system that Aikens and Vorgens had worked out. The Star Watchman smiled to himself. Both sides had been somewhat wary at the beginning, early in the morning, but now they seemed immersed in the problem. The Shinarians appeared especially impressed with the idea that they could defend themselves; no Terran had ever granted them that much before.

A communications tech popped his head up from the open hatch beside Vorgens.

'Message for you, sir.'

'What is it?'

'From the main body of the Force, sir. One of the natives was looking for you – that girl, the one that was with the priest.'

'Altai?'

'The exec spoke with her a few minutes ago. She seemed very agitated, he said, and was coming over here to see you. She's flying on a Komani vehicle, sir.'

Vorgens nodded absent-mindedly. What was wrong with Altai? Suddenly the tech's last words made an impression on him:

'Alert everyone in the area that a single Komani flyer will be coming in. I don't want anyone firing at it . . . especially those eager recruits down by the woods.'

The tech arched his eyebrows and nodded. 'Yes sir.' He disappeared inside the hatch.

Vorgens' face knitted into a frown. Something was wrong. *Altai isn't the type that panics – but she's flying here to see me – instead of using the tri-di. Something is very wrong.*

Yet, strangely, he felt pleased that she was coming to him. No matter what the trouble was, he would be glad to see her.

About a half-hour later, a lone Komani flyer whizzed over the meadow, then slowed and spiralled down lower. Vorgens could see Altai's hair streaming in the wind. She spotted the Watchman, and put the flyer down beside the troop carrier.

Vorgens clambered down from the groundcar as she ran up toward him.

'It's Merdon,' she said breathlessly, before he could ask anything. 'He's gone wild. Okatar is sending a column of troops to sack Katan – where his father lives. Merdon is gathering up as many men as he can to attack Okatar's main camp and kill him.'

It took Vorgens a moment to digest the news. 'But that's insane,' he said finally. 'The camp is too heavily guarded for him to get through. It's a suicide mission, and it won't help his father in Katan.'

Altai nodded. 'Katan is too far away to be reached in time. The Komani troops will be there tomorrow morning, at the latest. Even if Merdon had enough groundcars for his men, he couldn't be there until late in the afternoon. What can we do? He'll kill himself!'

Vorgens looked at her. Altai's lovely face was twisted with worry over Merdon.

'Has he at least told his father about the attack?'

'I – I think so. Oh, he was so furious! He was raging. I've never seen him like this before.'

'It's all right. He has a temper and he uses it. It saves strain on his nervous system.'

151

'But what are we going to do?' she pleaded. 'What can we do?'

Vorgens grinned at her. 'First, we can calm down and try to think straight. Second, can that flying machine carry the two of us?'

'Um . . . yes, I imagine so. It's built to carry Komani warriors, and neither of us is much more than half their weight.'

'Good. Let's go back to my headquarters. We've got work to do.'

'And that's the way I see it, brigadier,' Vorgens said.

Aikens was sitting across the table from the Watchman, in the dreadnaught's officers' wardroom. A pair of majors and the exec were also at the table. Steaming coffee mugs stood before each man.

Aikens had listened in dour silence to Vorgens' analysis of the situation. Now, he hunched forward in his chair and leaned his elbows on the green tabletop.

'Let me understand you clearly. You want to dispatch troops to Katan to beat off the Komani attack, and you expect me to devise a tactical plan of battle.' As usual, he placed a slight, sullen accent on the word *tactical*.

'First of all,' Vorgens answered, 'I want your opinion on whether we can beat off the Komani attack. I don't want to waste troops on a meaningless gesture.'

Aikens nodded. 'That's sensible. Based on what the observation planes from Capital City have reported, the Komani column should be at Katan by mid-morning tomorrow. The earliest we could get there would be mid-afternoon. So we can't stop their attack.'

'That's what I was afraid of.'

'But we can', Aikens went on, with a curious crooked smile, 'smash that column of savages just the same. Let them hit the city. Let them wreck it. Then we'll hit them when they're totally disorganized and unprepared for fighting.'

'But there wouldn't be much left of the city when we got through.'

Aikens shrugged. 'Perhaps the citizens could hold off the attackers for a few hours. You claim they're fighters.'

Vorgens let the brigadier's sarcasm slide past him. 'That

might work. I'll get in touch with Clanthas and see what he can organize in the way of a defense. In the meantime, your staff should draw up detailed battle plans. Determine how many troops you'll need and how much transport. Also, I'm going to dispatch a transport group for some of the natives who're willing to fight in defense of Katan.'

Aikens grunted noncommittally. 'I'll keep the few planes we have at Capital City in the air to watch the Komani.'

'Should you have them try to bomb the column – slow it down?'

The brigadier shook his head. 'No, the Komani are too spread out for nuclear weapons, and trying to go low and hit them with beams or missiles will just get the planes shot up. If we had more planes, or if these backward natives had some . . .'

'They're not backward. They just don't need aircraft,' Vorgens said. 'Groundcars can go almost as fast as subsonic planes, and they can carry considerably more payload. With groundcars, and tri-di communications, these people simply don't need fast fleets of aircraft.'

'Well, backward or not, they don't have what it takes,' Aikens said acidly. 'Now, if you'll excuse us, we have work to do.'

'Yes,' Vorgens said, rising from his chair, 'so do I.'

The Star Watchman hurried through the narrow passage-ways to the dreadnaught's communications center – that compact jumble of molectronic transceivers, coders, view-screens and recorders. Altai was there, talking quietly with the two technicians on duty. The techs seemed happily amazed at the chance to talk to a young, good-looking girl. As Vorgens stepped through the open hatch, though, they both shot out of their seats and stood at ramrod attention.

'Stand easy,' Vorgens said. Then, he asked Altai, 'Did you reach Clanthas?'

'Yes. Merdon had already called him, and advised him to abandon the city. Clanthas refused. He's organizing the people of Katan. They're going to fight for their city.'

'Good, we're going to help them.'

'What . . . what about Merdon?' she asked.

'Can he be reached by tri-di?'

Altai shook her head. 'I tried a few minutes ago. He's left the factory, where he had set up headquarters.'

Vorgens rubbed his temple thoughtfully. 'In that case,' he said, 'we'll have to go out and find him.' He turned to the techs. 'Get Sergeant McIntyre and tell him to have an aircar ready for us in ten minutes.'

'Yes sir.'

The Mobile Force had three aircars, used mainly for scouting. They took off vertically on jets of air blasted straight downward – somewhat similar to the method used to raise the groundcars above ground level. The aircars lifted for several hundred feet, though, and then the jet engines swiveled and moved the craft forward. Stubby wings provided all the necessary lift, and the craft could sprint at twice the speed of sound, when required.

'There they are, sir,' said the Marine pilot as they flew over Merdon's forces.

McIntyre, sitting in the gunner's seat, grunted. 'Not much of a force t' tackle th' whole Komani camp.'

Vorgens and Altai looked through the plastic bubble window as the pilot banked. Several hundred young men and girls were gathered on the grassy field below. Some were in trucks and small groundcars, most were afoot. They had plenty of small arms, but practically no heavy equipment. At the head of the loosely organized column was a light Terran armored groundcar.

'We captured that in the first battle at the university,' Altai explained. 'It is Merdon's prize possession.'

'Put us down in front of the armored car,' Vorgens told the pilot.

The aircar settled down swiftly, on screaming jets. As it touched the grass with its landing wheels, the armored car pulled up and stopped. The rest of the Shinarians slowly began to gather around, as Vorgens and Altai stepped down from the aircar, and Merdon, Tarat and Romal got out of the armored vehicle.

'We meet again,' Vorgens said.

'What are you doing here?' asked Merdon.

'I want to talk with you.'

'The time for talking is finished. Get out of our way. We have work to do.'

154

They stood face to face – the young, slim foreigner in his Star Watch uniform, and the equally young, slightly bigger native. They were nearly the same height, and almost the same complexion. From a distance, where you could not see the difference in clothing, they might seem to be brothers.

'Your mission can wait a few minutes, can't it?' Vorgens insisted. 'What I have to say is vitally important to all of us, including your father.'

The tenseness in Merdon's face relaxed a bit. 'All right. A few minutes.'

Vorgens looked around at the crowd that had gathered about them.

'Perhaps we could talk better up there.' He pointed to a little knoll.

Merdon shrugged.

'We're going for a walk, sergeant,' Vorgens told McIntyre, 'and I don't want to be disturbed.'

Merdon said much the same to Tarat. Then they started walking, in silence.

But as they reached the foot of the knoll and began climbing its gentle slope, Merdon asked: 'You talked with my father?'

'Altai did. He's organizing a defense of the city.'

'He'll get himself killed.'

'What are you going to do to help save him?'

Merdon glanced at the Watchman. 'There's nothing I can do. You know that. Katan is too far away, even for the fastest groundcars. The Komani will be there before we can get to the city.'

'So?'

Merdon stopped walking. 'So I'm going to hit the Komani where it will hurt the most. I'm going to kill Okatar.'

Vorgens pursed his lips thoughtfully. Then he said. 'That won't save your father.'

'He could save himself if he'd abandon the city.'

'Would you run away, if you were in his place?'

Merdon opened his mouth to answer, but no words came out.

'You may have heard,' Vorgens said, resuming his climb toward the top of the knoll, 'that my personal situation has changed somewhat since our last meeting.'

Merdon, striding swiftly to catch up with the Watchman, could not help grinning. 'I've heard.'

'I'm no longer a prisoner, and while my rank is still that of a junior officer, I am the Star Watch officer in command of Shinar.'

'I – I apologize for the way I treated you on our first meeting. I lost my temper.'

Vorgens plucked a leafy twig from the shrubbery. 'I accept your apology ... under one condition. I want you to hear me out.'

'I'm listening.'

'There are only three points I want to make. First: the Empire has not treated Shinar well. This is not because of Terran maliciousness; it's just an accidental by-product of the Imperial system. You could be treated much better under the Empire. Other worlds are.

'Second: Shinar is too small a world, and too weak militarily, to stand alone. If Imperial troops were not here fighting for your people – don't frown, that's what they're doing – if they weren't here to fight for your people, the Komani would be ruling you with a whip and a gun.

'Finally: Shinar can achieve its own internal freedom under the Empire. I'm saying *can*, not *will*. Other planets have done it. Perhaps yours can, too. It's something worth working toward, worth risking a lot for – it's even worth fighting for – because it's the only way you'll ever gain freedom.'

'What kind of freedom would it be?' Merdon asked, with quiet bitterness. 'The Terrans would still control us. They'd own our souls.'

'Don't be dramatic,' Vorgens said. 'The usual arrangement is to allow the planet complete internal freedom. You can rule yourselves in any way you see fit. The Empire would reserve the right to regulate your commercial treaties with other planets, but once a treaty is made, it's binding on the Empire as well as you. The Empire is ruled by law. You'd have all the legal rights that any other self-governing planet of the Empire enjoys.'

'You make it sound like Sittas' dreams of heaven.'

Vorgens laughed. 'No, it won't be heaven. While the Empire is ruled by law, it is still governed by men. There'll always be differences of opinion, problems, arguments. But you'd have as much of a chance to get your own way as anyone else would.'

They had reached the top of the knoll, and stood in knee-deep scrubgrass. A soft breeze moderated the heat of the sun. The deep blue, nearly violet, sky stood sparkling and cloudless all around them.

Vorgens stretched an arm toward the horizon. 'This is a good world, Merdon. A green world, filled with people who deserve a chance to live in peace.'

'They deserve freedom!' Merdon insisted. 'And they're willing to fight for it.'

Vorgens stepped over to the slightly taller Shinarian and grabbed him by the shoulders. 'Don't you understand, you hothead? I want them to be free! I want them to live their lives the way they want; to reach in any direction they choose; to be free from all outside domination.'

Merdon took a step backward, and Vorgens let his hands drop to his sides. Then he went on, 'They can do this under the Empire. It won't happen overnight, but they can achieve this freedom. Peacefully! What alternative to the Empire do you have? The Komani? Nonsense. Complete independence? You'd be swallowed up by more powerful neighbors within a year. Fine words and brave sentiments are perfectly good in their place, Merdon, but it takes more than that to achieve freedom. You must look at the real world, as it actually exists – not the world you would like to see, not your own dreams. In this real world, you must work for solutions that can be achieved.

'You can't solve all your problems with a wave of the hand,' Vorgens went on. 'You tried to do that by bringing the Komani to Shinar. What's happened? Chaos. No one's going to come to Shinar and grant you complete independence at a stroke, but under the Empire you have a better chance to achieve more freedom than any other way offers.'

Merdon scratched his head. 'Maybe you're right,' he admitted. 'I – I told Okatar he could name his own price if he would just leave Shinar and attack another Empire planet. Anything – all the equipment, food, ammunition he wanted – just to leave Shinar. It was a stupid thing to do. A wrong thing. His answer was – to take the offer, and at the same time attack Katan.'

'He wants to show you that you've been conquered,' Vorgens said.

'Right. To Okatar, we're already slaves. He'll take what he wants from us.'

'Unless we stop him.'

'And that's what I'm going to do,' Merdon concluded grimly.

'Not by attacking his camp,' Vorgens countered. 'All you'd accomplish there is your own death.'

'I've got to try!'

'Then try this: join us in the defense of Katan. Your father's organizing the citizens of the city. If he can hold out for a few hours, we can bring up Terran Marines, and your own forces, and crush the attackers.'

Merdon shook his head. 'Don't you think I've thought of that? I just don't have enough groundcars to get to Katan that quickly.'

Vorgens grinned. 'Don't *you* think *I've* thought of that? I can have a squadron of vans and troop carriers here within the hour.'

Merdon was silent for a moment. Then, looking straight into the Watchman's eyes, he said, 'I've been terribly wrong about a lot of things, but most of all about you. I'm going to tell my people to follow your orders. I'll stay behind – unless you – unless you're willing to have me fight alongside you.'

Vorgens said nothing, but put his hand out toward Merdon. The Shinarian smiled broadly, and took the Watchman's hand in a firm grasp. Then they went down, side by side, to the waiting people.

Clanthas was sitting out on the veranda again, watching the sun go down. For the first time in his life, he felt fear at the approach of night. Somewhere off in the rolling countryside, he knew, a column of Komani warriors was advancing on his city.

A Terran jet flew overhead, its engines barely audible at the great altitude it held, its contrail of 'frozen lightning' picking up the reddish glow of the dying sun. There was no airfield at Katan. The busy port city depended on groundcars and the huge, ocean-spanning transports that skimmed over land and sea with equal ease.

That was a Terran jet overhead. Strangely, it seemed to comfort the merchant. The Terrans were active. They were coming to the aid of Katan. But would they come soon enough? That was the question.

CHAPTER EIGHTEEN

THE RACE TO KATAN

Through the long night the people of Katan prepared for the oncoming Komani. The arsenal was opened and every citizen – male or female – old enough and strong enough to handle a weapon was issued one. The city's lights burned all night long as, building by building, block by block, people huddled together to make plans, to pick the best windows and rooftops to mount guns, to pray.

By dawn, they were ready. The usual early-morning bustle of commerce was replaced by a deadly, calm quiet. Shops and offices were closed. Windows and doors bolted. The streets were empty, except for a few patrolling policemen. The hot, yellow sun rose, the sparkling water lapped the harbor docks and seawalls, the morning breeze blew in from the ocean, but the citizens of Katan were not out of doors to see. They waited indoors, grimly checking their weapons and ammunition.

The city lay curving around its crescent-shaped harbor. A small river cut through the heart of Katan, dividing it into two unequal segments, called the Lesser City and the Greater City. Beyond the outskirts of the city, beyond the parks and playgrounds and occasional suburban estates, were the rolling, wooded hills that masked the approach of the Komani.

The lulling calm of the morning was shattered by the scream of an aircar streaking fast and low over the buildings. The plane circled twice, then made a vertical descent into a deserted public park in the residential section of the city.

A handful of policemen ran to the aircar as its jets whined to a stop. Guns poked out ominously from dozens of windows and rooftops. Vorgens, Aikens, McIntyre, and two of the brigadier's staff officers climbed out. The Shinarians relaxed. A groundcar slid up to the Terrans, and they were whisked to Clanthas' home.

Clanthas had turned his veranda into a battle headquarters. The town council, the mayor, the police chief and several other community leaders were there to greet the Terrans. Vorgens quickly introduced Brigadier Aikens, Sergeant McIntyre, and the brigadier's two aides.

'We passed over the Komani column,' the Watchman said before Clanthas could say anything. 'They're about two hours away – perhaps a little less.'

'And your troops?' the mayor asked.

'They're moving up in land cruisers,' Brigadier Aikens said, stepping between Vorgens and the mayor. 'Won't be here until noon, at the earliest. You must defend the city as best as possible until then.'

The mayor exchanged worried glances with the others.

'The brigadier has drawn up a plan of action,' Vorgens said.

'Do you have a map of the city?' Aikens asked Clanthas.

The merchant smiled. 'Better than that . . . I have the city itself.'

Clanthas led them around the veranda to the side that faced away from the harbor. The entire group clustered around Aikens as he looked out over the rooftops of Katan.

'I see what you mean,' the brigadier said. 'An excellent view. Now then, that large square building down there, across the river . . .' He pointed. 'That's the arsenal, isn't it?'

Clanthas nodded.

Aikens turned and leaned slightly over the railing. 'And down on this side . . . those are the warehouses?'

'Yes, along the waterfront of the Lesser City.'

Aikens grunted with satisfaction. 'All right. Now, the arsenal and the warehouses will be the two principal objectives of the Komani.'

'The arsenal will be practically useless to them,' Clanthas said, 'since we have distributed almost all the weapons and ammunition to our people.'

'Good! I was counting on that. We'll let the Komani spend some time and effort taking the arsenal, but we won't defend that end of the city very strongly. Evacuate your people and leave only a thin screen of men; fight a rearguard action.'

The mayor gasped. 'You mean that we should allow them to take half the Greater City? But the factories, the business district, the homes . . .'

'They have no military value,' Aikens snapped. 'You're fighting for time, with untrained rabble facing tough, battle-tested troops. You can't hold the entire city. You've got to pick out the part that you *must* defend, and let the Komani have the rest, temporarily.'

'But they'll loot it . . . destroy everything.'

Aikens planted his fists on his hips. 'Listen! I'm here to save your necks and to defeat the Komani. I'm not going to worry about real estate values.'

Vorgens added, more softly, 'If all goes well, the Komani won't have much time for looting. Besides, the buildings would be damaged much more severely if heavy fighting took place in them.'

The mayor shook his head. 'I suppose so.'

'All right then,' Aikens resumed, turning slightly away from the Watchman. 'The warehouses will be defended. We'll set up a firm line of resistance a few blocks in front of them. And we'll also set up a flanking line along the river.'

'The river is no barrier to Komani mounted on flyers,' Vorgens pointed out.

Aikens smiled icily, and with an obvious patience, explained, 'No, but it's a moderately wide open space, with no buildings to provide shelter. If they try to fly across the river, they'll be putting themselves in the middle of a firing range.'

'Good,' Clanthas said, sensing the hostility between the two men and trying to change the subject before it broke out into the open. 'What else?'

'Three companies of Imperial Marines are being flown here by jet. They should arrive momentarily.'

'But we have no airfield.'

'They'll jump from the planes and come down on jet-belts. When our task unit from the Mobile Force arrives we'll be able to drive the Komani out of the city – if all goes well this morning.'

'Very well,' Clanthas said. He turned to the mayor, 'We must inform our people about this plan of battle. We have to move swiftly.'

Within a moment, the veranda was deserted, except for the Terrans.

'They seemed to accept your plan,' Vorgens said to the brigadier.

'They'd better.'

Sergeant McIntyre asked the Watchman, 'Sir, when the airborne troops get here, they'll need somebody t' show 'em where they're supposed t' set up . . . won't they?'

'Very well, Sergeant,' Vorgens said, 'you may report to the brigade commander. I didn't think I'd be able to keep you out of the fighting.'

McIntyre saluted briskly. 'Thank you, sir!'

Aikens said, 'If you're going back to the Mobile Force, Watchman, you'd better start off right away. There's not much time left before the shooting starts.'

Vorgens met the older man's eyes. 'When are you leaving?'

'When the battle's done.'

'Then I'll stay too, if you don't mind.'

They stood facing each other in silence for a moment. Then Aikens turned away.

'Look!' shouted one of the brigadier's aides. 'The jets.'

They could see three fine, white contrails hurrying across the morning sky. Within minutes, the planes had come low enough to flood the city with the thunder of their engines. Tiny figures began to jump from them, with crisp military precision, and float slowly downward.

Vorgens turned away and looked at the hills. Wordlessly, he reached out and tapped Aikens' shoulder. The brigadier turned and stared in the direction of Vorgens' gaze.

Coming over the hills, like a dark cloud of angry locusts, was the swarm of Komani flyers.

It was not pretty to watch a city being destroyed.

Vorgens stood at his post on the veranda, within earshot of the communications center that Aikens had set up, and saw the battle unfold.

The Komani split into two columns. One bore straight down on the Lesser City, driving for the warehouses by the waterfront. The other swung wide across the open suburban greenery and attacked the Greater city, aiming for the arsenal.

By noontime, the bright sunshine was blotted out by a pall of smoke rising from dozens of fires raging through Katan. Vorgens could see that most of the Greater City was a shambles. The Komani had slashed their way easily to the arsenal, and when they found it nearly empty, had turned their frustrated rage to the building itself. They set it ablaze, and then fanned out through the Greater City, looting, burning, destroying. Now the arsenal was a blackened, gutted shell, and the buildings around it smoldered also.

But all this was secondary to the fierce battle flaring through the streets of the Lesser City.

The Komani column driving toward the warehouses had met stiff resistance from the citizens of Katan and from the hastily assembled brigade of Marines. Aikens' defensive perimeter, drawn up a few blocks in front of the warehouses and swinging around to follow the riverside flank, had temporarily stopped the Komani onslaught.

The fighting had slowed down to a bitter, house-to-house, man-to-man struggle. Most of the Komani had dismounted from their flyers and fought now on foot. A few still remained aloft, though, to pepper rooftops and windows. Clanthas' veranda had been buzzed several times. Vorgens now held a beam pistol in his hand.

Although they were outnumbered, the Komani were relentlessly pressing their attack home. They had quickly learned to stay out of the buildings, where a dozen Shinarians could surprise a lone invader. Now they were boring through the streets and over rooftops, routing the city's defenders with superior discipline and the dispassionate courage that comes from long experience in battle.

Three times Aikens had to move his core of Imperial Marines backwards, because the Komani had penetrated the streets on their flanks and threatened to surround them. Now they were fighting in the square that opened onto the warehouse district.

Vorgens could see, too, that the Komani sacking the Greater City must have received word of the heavy fighting going on near the warehouses. They had stopped their senseless looting and burning, and were forming up in the streets.

The Watchman ducked around a corner of the veranda to Aikens at his makeshift communications center. The brigadier had taken one side of the veranda and filled it with technicians, aides, and equipment.

He was leaning over one of the techs, barking orders into

164

a viewscreen. Vorgens touched his arm. The brigadier straightened and turned to the Watchman.

'In another moment or two,' Vorgens said, 'the warriors from the Greater City will be flying here to help their friends.'

'I know!' Aikens snapped. 'What do you think I'm trying to do here, organize a tea party? I'm setting up a lane of fire on both sides of the river. We'll cut down as many of 'em as possible before they can join the attack here.'

'What about our task unit from the Mobile Force?' Vorgens asked.

'They're on their way.'

It was almost two hours more before the Terrans finally arrived.

The three companies of air-dropped Marines had been whittled down to a stubborn handful, fighting tenaciously at the steps of the warehouses they were defending. Shinarians – old men, boys, women among them – fought and died alongside the Imperial troops.

All along the river Komani warriors were darting wildly on their utterly maneuverable flyers, trying to avoid the withering fire coming up from both banks. Some of the flyers got through, and went on to join the attack on the warehouses. Most of the others had turned back though, and were blasting the buildings from which the Shinarians fired.

A squad of flying Komani warriors had fought its way to the roof of one warehouse when Vorgens saw the first Terran troop carriers racing over the final row of hills before the city.

The Watchman turned to Aikens, and saw that the brigadier was still immersed in crackling out orders to his men. Beyond the brigadier's shoulder, Vorgens could see more battle cruisers skimming over the harbor water, heading for the warehouses at top speed. Only then did he realize that the vehicles coming in from the hills carried Merdon's men, not Marines.

The Komani were caught in a vise.

Aikens' Marines, in battle cruisers and armored cars, drove up the streets between the warehouses, crushing the Komani attack with massed firepower. The invading warriors fell back, slowly at first, but when they tried to regroup, they found Terran armored vehicles boring down on them. The Komani fled for the city's outskirts, only to be met by Merdon's vengeful fighters.

By nightfall it was ended. A few of the attackers had escaped – very few. Merdon and the exhausted citizens of Katan rejoiced by torchlight through the blackened, rubble-strewn streets.

Vorgens remained at the railing of the veranda, watching the celebration, in the dark. The city's electrical power generators had been heavily damaged.

'Sir.'

He turned, and in the flickering shadows saw McIntyre, grimy and tired, but alive. 'You've – done a good day's work, Sergeant.'

A satisfied grin broke across McIntyre's beefy face. 'Thank you sir. Uh – we're just about ready t' leave. The brigadier has already gone back t' the Mobile Force. All other troops have pulled out.'

'All right,' Vorgens said quietly. 'I suppose there's no sense in my staying any longer.'

McIntyre peered out over the railing. 'They're havin' some time down there – celebratin' their victory. I – uh, don't suppose we could stay a bit longer and join 'em?'

'Victory?' the Watchman echoed. 'What victory? Look at this city. It's smashed to pieces. Who won?'

McIntyre shrugged. 'They seem t' think *they* won, sir. They're already talkin' about how they're gonna rebuild the damaged sections of town.'

Vorgens did not answer. He started toward the stairs that led down to the courtyard before Clanthas' home and the aircar waiting there. Someone was coming up the steps. Altai.

'Here you are!' she said to Vorgens.

'I'm on my way back to the Mobile Force,' he said.

'Leaving? But why?'

'Why not? The battle's over. Your people want to celebrate. You'll want to get back to Merdon and the others.'

She smiled and stepped closer to him. 'I haven't said more than six words to Merdon since yesterday, and I'm not joining the celebration until you come with me. They're celebrating their freedom, and you're the man responsible for it. You're coming with me!'

166

'I . . .'

Devilishly, she added, 'You wouldn't want Merdon to get *all* the credit, would you? Come on!'

Vorgens grinned back at her. 'All right, you win. Sergeant, I guess we'll be staying awhile longer.'

'Yes *sir*,' McIntyre said happily.

CHAPTER NINETEEN

ATTRITION

The celebration at Katan was followed by six weeks of virtually uninterrupted battle flaming across the breadth of Shinar. Okatar Kang had decided to sack the planet, relentlessly raiding every district, every town, systematically taking all the food, weapons, equipment and ammunition he desired.

Opposed to the Komani plan stood Vorgens and his concept of Shinarian self-defense, directed and keystoned by the Terrans.

It was a peculiar battle in many ways. Instead of large masses of troops and weapons clashing head-on, there were skirmishes, maneuverings, feints, sudden vicious attacks, ambushes – few single actions involved more than a battalion of men.

Vorgens worked constantly, almost without rest, living on stimulants, cajoling Aikens, persuading the Shinarians to trust the Terrans.

With the Shinarians taking over a good part of their own defense, and with Merdon's fighters providing reconnaissance and intelligence, the Terrans were able to meet the Komani on their own terms. When a Komani raiding party headed for a town, it would be intercepted by a fast, strong squadron of battle cruisers. Farming villages became little fortresses dotting the countryside, often with a Terran dreadnaught camped in the village square. Komani columns were ambushed. When Okatar massed his strength and tried to force a pitched battle, he found that the Terrans could also disperse and disappear into the countryside.

The Komani still outnumbered the Imperial troops on Shinar. But whenever the Terrans struck, they usually had superior strength at that particular place for that brief time.

It was a war of attrition, with fatigue and hunger and mechanical breakdown playing as important a role as weapons.

'We're failing,' Vorgens said tiredly. 'We're failing miserably.'

He was sitting at the head of the green-covered table in the officer's wardroom of the command dreadnaught. Grouped around the table were Merdon, Brigadier Aikens, the exec, Sergeant McIntyre, and a few other officers.

'I wouldn't say that, Watchman,' the brigadier objected. 'We're holding our own against the barbarians.'

'We've beaten off most of their attacks. The people are learning to defend themselves,' Merdon agreed.

Vorgens shook his head. 'The best we can say is that we've accomplished a stalemate. Our objective is peace. We have perpetual fighting. That's failure.'

'What do you propose?' the exec asked.

'That's the worst part of it – I can't see any clear way out,' Vorgens admitted. 'Either the Komani will remain here until one side or the other collapses from exhaustion, or – worse still – Okatar will pull his clan off Shinar and attack another planet. Then the whole bloody business will be repeated again.'

'What about the reinforcements on their way here?' Aikens asked.

'They won't be enough to make much difference,' Vorgens said. 'In fact, just because they're so few, they'll verify Okatar's claim that the Empire can't defend Shinar adequately. Those reinforcements might lead to strengthening Okatar's hand! Other Komani clans might be tempted to join him when they see how weak the Empire's response is.'

A gloomy silence settled over them.

Finally, Merdon said, 'I know a way of breaking this deadlock.'

Everyone turned to him.

'Kill Okatar,' Merdon said simply. 'Decapitate the Komani clan.'

Aikens grunted. 'You'd never be able to get to him.'

'It would just make the Komani fight harder,' the exec said.

'That would be barbaric,' Vorgens said. 'To deliberately plan a man's death . . .'

'This is war,' Aikens snapped. 'Every one of us runs the risk of being killed.'

'In battle, yes,' Vorgens countered. 'But not in bed. No, I can't condone assassination.'

'But if it were done,' Merdon insisted, 'it would break the stalemate, wouldn't it?'

'Possibly. I don't know. It would certainly throw the Komani into confusion, at least temporarily. Perhaps then they might be willing to talk about peace . . .'

Merdon changed the subject then, and the conference droned on for another fruitless hour. No decision was reached. The Terrans and Shinarians would continue to fight as they had been fighting for more than six weeks. The war of attrition would go on.

In the passageway outside the wardroom, Merdon grasped Sergeant McIntyre's arm and asked, 'Can we talk for a moment?'

The sergeant nodded, and the two of them walked slowly down the passageway. McIntyre loomed bulkily next to the slim Shinarian youth.

'What do you think about the chances of getting to Okatar?' Merdon asked in a half-whisper.

McIntyre shrugged. 'It's a big camp – hard t' get into. And even harder t' get out of.'

'Listen,' Merdon whispered, suddenly intense, 'I know every blade of grass in the camp. I can get six men through the guards and into Okatar's tent. I've been planning this for weeks, and I know it can be done!'

The sergeant rubbed his massive jaw. 'How d' you get 'em away afterwards?'

'Jetbelts.'

'Might work.'

'I need six men trained in silent night fighting.'

'Five, countin' me,' said Sergeant McIntyre.

Three nights later, they made their try.

McIntyre had recruited five Marines, including Giradaux. The lanky young trooper had sensed that the sergeant was up to something, and had forced McIntyre to take him along, as the price of silence.

A driving rainstorm had blown up from the south, predicted by the Terran meteorologists. Merdon was counting on the storm to provide a cover of darkness against the usual twilight glow of the Shinarian night.

They commandeered a scoutcar and started off cross-country, guided by the car's infra-red lamps. Ordinary light would have been detected too easily, both by the Komani and the occasional Terran patrols.

McIntyre drove, with Merdon in the skipper's seat directing him. The five troopers sat in dark silence amidst their jetbelts, guns and grenades, listening to the whine of the car's engine and the rain pelting the armored roof just above their helmets.

'There's the forest coming up,' Merdon said, pointing into the viewscreen in front of McIntyre. 'You won't be able to take the car very deep into it.'

McIntyre nodded as he eased up on the throttle. 'I'll put 'er in a little ways, so she'll be under cover.'

Within a few minutes, the seven of them were slogging through the rain-soaked woods.

It took nearly two hours of steady marching through the angry rain before they cleared the forest and saw the edge of the Komani camp.

Crouching in the bushes at the forest's edge, Merdon scanned the camp with infra-red binoculars.

'Only a few guards,' he muttered, 'and plenty of open space between them. The camp is almost completely blacked out. The rain has even put out the ceremonial fires.'

'Don't they have automatic detection equipment that sets off an alarm as soon as somebody crosses th' energy screen?' McIntyre asked.

'No. That's a Terran refinement that the Komani don't have. Guards with snooperscopes . . . that's what they use. Believe me, it'll be tough enough to get through them.'

They skirted along the edge of the encampment, looking for their best opening. At last they found a spot where the foliage nearly reached the energy screen. There were only about twenty yards of open space between the forest shrubbery and the nearest Komani tents.

They waited for the guard to make a couple of rounds, so they could time his approach. Then they started crawling – two at a time – for the tents. McIntyre and Giradaux were the first pair to start. The rain had slackened a little but was

171

still heavy enough to be troublesome. For what seemed like hours, the two Marines inched along on their stomachs, while the others covered them with their guns.

Merdon was the last to go across. He pulled himself along the wet, slippery grass and mud, his vision restricted to the same view of the world that a worm might have.

Suddenly he heard McIntyre's harsh whisper in his helmet earphones. 'Freeze!'

Merdon stopped dead and buried his face in his arms. He was wearing a black uniform and equipment, as the Marines were. But still it seemed his heart was pounding loud enough to be heard all over the camp.

Finally McIntyre whispered, 'Okay.'

The young Shinarian slithered across the last remaining yards and joined the others in the relative safety behind the tents.

'What happened?' he asked as they helped him to his feet.

'Changing of the guard,' McIntyre answered. 'Two of 'em walked right out in fronta you. Lucky they didn't look your way.'

Merdon grinned. 'Well let's get moving while our luck still holds.'

They made their way as quickly as possible toward the center of the camp. Merdon pointed the way, and McIntyre directed their movements. The seven of them fanned out slightly, but still kept within sight of each other. One man would move ahead the distance of a single tent, make certain the way was clear, then signal the next man to move up. They kept to the shadows, and their guns were always in their hands, ready to fire.

Four times they had to stop, as guards crossed their path, treading sleepily through the darkened camp. Once a guard started to walk directly toward a pair of Marines, crouching alongside a tent. McIntyre sprang at the Komani's back and felled him with a savage chop at the neck.

'Is he dead?' Merdon whispered.

'Dunno . . . but he'll be out for a good long time, at least.'

'Come on,' Merdon said. 'The rain's slackening. It's starting to brighten up a little.'

Finally they reached Okatar's golden dome. Light was streaming from the main entrance.

'There are two other entrances, on the other side of the tent,' Merdon said.

McIntyre nodded to his men. 'Two of you take each entrance. Gerry, you and Merdon come with me, through the main gate. Now get this straight, all of you: no Komani leaves that tent alive. Understand?'

They nodded.

The four Marines disappeared into the shadows. McIntyre hunched down into a squat and surveyed the tent's main entrance. A pair of guards stood tiredly leaning on their rifles.

'How many Komani will be inside?' the sergeant asked.

Merdon shrugged. 'It depends. If Okatar has his full council in there, it might be twenty-five or thirty men.'

The Marines at the other two entrances signaled through their helmet radios that they were ready.

'Okay,' McIntyre whispered. *Now!*'

He got both the guards with a single sweeping blast from his beam rifle as they dashed out of the shadows and toward the entrance.

Inside, the tent suddenly looked deserted – a single large area, richly decorated and furnished – but empty of Komani. Then a grenade went off, somewhere on the other side of the tent.

'The council chamber,' Merdon shouted as he ran toward the far end of the room.

Before they could get to the doorway, a trio of Komani nobles bolted through it and faced them. Merdon cut them down with his beam pistol before they could change the surprised expressions on their faces.

Inside the council chamber, one of the Marines was sprawled limply over an ornate chair, while another was kneeling beside him, firing at five Komani who had taken shelter behind the massive council table. The farther end of the table was splintered and blackened from a grenade's blast. McIntyre pushed behind a chair and up to the table itself, then sprayed the length of it with the highest-power beam he could get from his rifle. The table flashed into flames, forcing the Komani back away from it. Within less than a minute they were all mowed down.

'Okatar's not here,' Merdon shouted. 'Come on, we've got to find him.'

They dashed through several other rooms, while the three surviving Marines took up defensive stations at each of the three entrances to the tent.

The rooms were empty. Smoke was starting to crawl ominously around them.

'The whole camp'll be in here in a minute!' McIntyre shouted.

Merdon said, 'He's got to be . . . LOOK OUT!'

Nearly a dozen Komani burst out of a doorway off to their right. Their first shots knocked down both McIntyre and Merdon, but Giradaux hurled a grenade into them before ducking behind a low-slung table. The concussion flattened everything in the room.

McIntyre was the first to recover. He rolled over onto his stomach and pulled the pistol from his belt. But none of the Komani were moving. Merdon climbed stiffly to his feet, the right side of his tunic showing a spreading stain of blood.

He pointed with his pistol. 'This one – here in the middle – that was Okatar.'

McIntyre pulled himself up. There was an ugly gash along the side of his head. 'Okay,' he said. 'Let's get outta here.'

The tent was filling with smoke now, and they could hear the shouts of fighting men approaching. The three Marines were still at the entrance, but two of them obviously were badly wounded.

'I'll get 'em,' Giradaux said. He touched the control stud at his waist that activated his jetbelt and rocketed across the room to the first of the wounded men. The trooper hurled his last grenade at the oncoming Komani, then took off on his own jetbelt and started toward McIntyre.

The sergeant and Merdon had joined the one unhurt Marine, at the entrance he was holding. Flames were licking up the side of the tent, and the Komani were beginning to organize their frantic, helter-skelter attempts to recapture the tent.

Before Giradaux could reach the other wounded Marine, the trooper keeled over and a horde of Komani boiled into the room.

Without an instant's hesitation, Giradaux jetted straight upward, sliced open the tent's dome with his beamgun as he flew, and disappeared through the roof.

Merdon took off at the same instant, leaping through the entrance and spiralling up around the tent's curving dome. McIntyre grabbed the wounded Marine and started to follow the Shinarian, but the trooper had collapsed and could not control his jetbelt. McIntyre hesitated for a moment – just long enough for a Komani warrior to reach him with a ceremonial broadsword gleaming wickedly in his upraised hand.

CHAPTER TWENTY

THE BOLDEST STEP

Vorgens did not notice that McIntyre was missing until the following morning. It took a little while for him to discover that the sergeant was nowhere in the Mobile Force, that Merdon and a few Marines were also gone, and that a scout car had disappeared.

The Watchman summoned Brigadier Aikens to the dreadnaught's wardroom. In cold fury, Vorgens explained the situation to him.

'I have only one question,' Vorgens concluded, barely able to keep his voice calm. 'Did you authorize this raid in which they must be engaged?'

'Raid?' Aikens asked.

'On the Komani camp,' Vorgens snapped. 'Did you authorize it?'

Aikens laughed. 'Until just now I didn't even know about it.'

'I see . . .'

The wall communicator chimed, and a trooper's face took form on the viewscreen. 'Sir, there's a trooper here at hatch four who demands to see you. Name of Giradaux. He says . . .'

'Send him here at once,' Vorgens said.

It took a minute for Giradaux to get from the outside hatch to the wardroom. He stepped wearily through the doorway, ducking his head to get his tall, lanky frame through. He looked utterly bedraggled. His uniform was caked with mud. His face was hollow-eyed and grimy. His shoulders slumped dejectedly. He didn't bother to salute. 'We got him for you,' he said to Vorgens.

'Got him?'

'Okatar. He's dead. I hope that makes you happy.'

'What are you . . .'

'We got Okatar,' the trooper said, his eyes filling with tears, 'and they got th' Sarge. Four killed, one wounded –

sir. Trooper Martinis and I weren't touched. It's a big victory for you – sir. A big victory.'

'McIntyre was killed?'

'That's right.' Giradaux answered, his voice rising. 'Did you expect any of us to come back alive?'

'I didn't even know . . .'

'You knew he'd try it. You must have known. He's dead, and you—'

'That's *enough!*' Aikens bellowed.

Giradaux snapped to attention.

'Get to your quarters, trooper. And don't budge a toe out of them until you're told to. *Move.*'

With deliberate care, Giradaux made a letter-perfect salute. Aikens returned it, and the trooper pivoted on his heel and left the wardroom. But Vorgens could still feel the pain that he felt, and sensed the anger within him.

'Whatever possessed a veteran like McIntyre to – to ignore my wishes, to go dashing off on his own?'

Aikens smiled grimly. 'An army is built on discipline, Watchman. McIntyre saw that discipline shattered the day you took over command. He was simply following the example you set – and you see where it leads.'

Vorgens sat in stunned silence as Aikens got up from his chair and strode out of the wardroom. He remained there, alone, heedless of time, staring at the bare, metal wall with unseeing eyes. Officers and orderlies would open the door to the wardroom from time to time, and, seeing him there and the expression on his face, would silently shut the door and leave Vorgens to himself.

Finally, the exec stepped in, hesitated a moment at the door, then walked to the chair next to Vorgens and sat down. He placed a yellow dispatch film on the tabletop before the Watchman.

'The ships from Star Watch Headquarters have arrived and taken up a parking orbit around the planet. When do you want the troops to land?'

Vorgens blinked, and focused his thoughts on the exec's question with an obvious effort.

'Tonight,' he said at last. 'Tell them to land under cover of darkness. I don't want the Komani to see how few they are.'

177

The exec nodded. 'Sir – I've been thinking. We could run the landing ships up and down as many times as you wish. They don't have to have a full load of troops on board. They can just shuttle back and forth between the starships and the planet all day long, if you like. The Komani won't know.'

'That would only fool them temporarily,' Vorgens said.

'Yes, I suppose so.'

'Is there anything else?'

'That – uh, that girl, sir. Altai. She's been waiting to see you.'

'No, I don't want to see anyone.'

'Sir, she's been waiting almost all day.'

'Oh? What time is it?'

'Nearly dark, sir.'

'I – I didn't realize that I'd been here so long.' He ran a weary hand across his eyes. 'All right, I suppose I'll have to see her sooner or later. Send her in.'

'Yes sir.'

'Oh . . . and release Trooper Giradaux from his quarters,' Vorgens called out as the exec headed for the door. 'He's to resume his normal duties.'

'Very well, sir.'

The exec opened the door, stepped through, and held it open for Altai. Vorgens rose and stood at the head of the table as she walked across the compact little room to him.

'I – I just realized that I don't know if Merdon's dead or alive,' the Watchman said.

'He's in the infirmary,' Altai said, sitting down next to Vorgens. 'He lost quite a bit of blood, but otherwise he's not in serious condition.'

Vorgens sat down and said nothing.

'Merdon told me that the plan was his,' she went on. 'He takes full responsibility for it.'

The Watchman shook his head. 'No. I'm in command. Whatever happens is my responsibility.'

'But you didn't know.'

'I should have. I might have guessed at it. I know Merdon doesn't give up an idea so easily. I gave McIntyre the impression that only Okatar's death could save us from continual fighting. He gave up his life at my suggestion, not Merdon's.'

178

'But you can't blame yourself for everything that happens on Shinar. That's wrong!'

'I blame myself for what happened last night, and for a lot more besides. As I look back on it, I realize how foolish I've been. I was going to bring peace to Shinar – single-handedly, if necessary! What a joke. All I've brought is pain and death and unending fighting.' He ran a hand over his close-cropped hair. There were hollows under his eyes, and his voice sounded husky.

'But you – I . . .' Suddenly Altai was tongue-tied. 'Do you have a first name?' she blurted. 'I can't call you Vorgens, or Watchman.'

In spite of himself, he smiled. '*Ehml'n*, in my native language. The Terrans find it easier to say Emil.'

'All right – Emil. Don't you realize how much you've done for Shinar – for all of us?'

He shook his head.

'You're blaming yourself for all the killing that's taken place here. That's wrong! Thanks to you, the men who've died have put a meaning to the deaths. They're accomplishing something that only you have allowed them to do.'

'Yes,' Vorgens replied. 'Only me.'

She reached out and grasped his hands on the tabletop. 'You've given us something to fight for – not the dream of complete freedom that Merdon wanted. Most of the people never believed that such a dream was possible. That's why Merdon's followers were only among the young. You've taught us that we may be able to gain real freedom within the Empire.'

'That might be an even wilder dream than Merdon's,' Vorgens said.

She smiled at him. 'You don't believe that, and neither do I. You've shown us that Terrans and Shinarians can work together. You've proved to us that we can think and act for ourselves, that we can defend our homes when necessary. Not by calling in warriors from another land – but by our-selves.

'And you've shown me,' she said more softly, 'that a man who hates fighting is a much better man to follow than someone who has learned to enjoy it.'

'That's – very kind of you,' he said, looking into her deep, dark eyes. 'In all the bitterness and bloodshed of these past months, the only touch of warmth and brightness has been you. Knowing you was almost worth all the rest.'

'Was?'

'I've decided to leave Shinar. There are Star Watch officers aboard the ships carrying our reinforcements. Anyone of them would be much better qualified to command the Imperial forces here than I am.'

'No! You can't. They wouldn't know the situation here the way you do. And how can our people trust a total stranger?'

'What else can I do?'

'Finish the work that you started out to do! You're the only man who has the grasp and the courage to try. Don't give up now. Keep working to bring peace to Shinar. Finish the work that we've all given so much to – especially your sergeant.'

'Do you really think it might be possible?'

'It has to be,' Altai insisted. 'With Okatar gone now, who knows what will happen next?'

'The next step,' Vorgens muttered, half to himself, 'probably depends on us.'

She said nothing, but sat back and watched his face as he thought over the alternatives.

Suddenly Vorgens got up from his chair and strode to the communicator on the wall near the door. He punched out a call number on the directory buttons. The exec's face showed up on the viewscreen.

'Please send my compliments to the commander of the relief ships in orbit,' the Watchman said, 'and ask him to delay landing the troops until full daylight at Capital City. The troops are to be landed just outside the city. And your idea about running the shuttles an extra few times to impress the Komani sounds good. Keep the landing ships running all day.'

'Yes, *sir*,' the exec replied, grinning.

'And another thing – I want an aircar for tomorrow morning, with a volunteer pilot. The car must be painted white.'

Thus the boldest step of all in the struggle for Shinar was begun.

Vorgens should have been surprised to see Giradaux standing at attention beside the white-painted aircar, but somehow he was not.

'You volunteered to pilot me?' the Watchman asked as he stepped up to the craft. He spoke softly enough so that the officers and men standing nearby would not overhear.

'Yes sir,' Giradaux answered, looking straight ahead. 'I wanted to – well – to make up for what I said yesterday, sir.'

Vorgens nodded. 'I understand.'

Brigadier Aikens joined them. 'If this pilot isn't satisfactory . . .'

'He'll do,' Vorgens said.

'You're still determined to go through with this?'

The Watchman nodded. 'Military action has taken us about as far as we can expect. It's time to try a political stroke.'

Aikens frowned distastefully. 'You probably won't get through this alive.'

'Perhaps,' Vorgens admitted cheerfully, 'but that would be no great loss to you, would it?'

Before the brigadier could reply, Vorgens swung up the access ladder and climbed into the aircar's open cabin. Giradaux trotted around to the other side, got in, and pulled down the plastic bubble top. The turbines growled into life, spraying dust around the base of the little craft. Aikens and the other men backed away as the car climbed slowly, its engines rising in pitch as its altitude increased. Finally the engines tilted forward, and the aircar shot ahead through the morning sky.

Aikens shook his head as the car disappeared from sight. 'We'll never see them again,' he said to the exec.

Vorgens spent most of the time aloft looking at the tri-di viewscreen on the control panel before him. He was watching the Imperial reinforcements land, just outside Capital City. A half-dozen needle-sleek, silvery landing ships were sitting tail-down on the plain and disgorging Marines. As he watched, two more settled down slowly, making the ground beneath them shimmer in the haze of their gray fields. Another ship took off, rising slowly, catching the morning sun on her gleaming hull.

It was an impressive sight, even though the actual number of Marines was quite small.

Finally Giradaux touched his arm and said, 'There it is, sir.'

Vorgens followed the trooper's gaze and saw the Komani camp.

A ring of ceremonial fires, spaced every fifty yards or so, circled the perimeter of the vast encampment. The gaudy domed tents were decked with blood-red drapings. Long processions of men, women and children were filing among the tents, heading for the center, where the dead Kang lay.

In the place where Okatar's golden tent had stood there now rose a tall pyre, unlit as yet. Heaped atop it were piles of offerings – weapons, ornaments, warriors' trappings, personal treasures – glittering in the sunshine. Vorgens could see the processions of Komani all converged on this pyre. Each person, no matter how young or old, handed something to the warriors who were stacking the offerings on the wooden structure that held the dead Kang's coffin.

Suddenly the sky around them was black with Komani flyers, buzzing angrily all around. Vorgens held up his hands in the sign of peace.

One of the Komani pulled up close enough to touch the aircar, and for several moments they flew side by side, staring at each other. Finally the warrior touched a jeweled band at his throat and then pointed to his lips.

'Try the radio,' Vorgens said to Giradaux.

'Leave here at once,' the warrior was snarling, 'and be grateful that we do not kill on a day of mourning. Only our ancient custom has saved your lives today.'

Vorgens replied evenly, 'I have come to pay my respects to your chieftain. I would like to land in your camp, and do him what little honor I can.'

The warrior looked thunderstruck. 'You dare to suggest that you should be allowed to – to . . .' He sputtered with rage.

'Do you dare,' Vorgens asked calmly, 'to refuse an honor to your Kang? How many chieftains have had an enemy leader ask to see their pyre?'

The warrior hesitated. Finally he said. 'This is not for me to decide. The council must make the choice.'

For nearly an hour, the Terran aircar circled slowly over the camp, with its sullen escort of Komani flyers.

'You're depending an awful lot on their customs, ain'tcha, sir?' Giradaux asked.

'They're ruled by custom,' the Watchman replied. *At least, that's what they told us at the Academy.*

At last the warrior told them to follow him to a landing. They put down in a cleared area near the edge of the camp. A knot of elders stood there, solemn and hostile, as Vorgens climbed down from the aircar.

'I am Lensor,' said one of the Komani, a grizzled, wrinkled nobleman, slightly stooped with age. Still he towered above the Watchman. 'Until a new Kang is chosen, I am leader of the council. By what right do you presume to interrupt our sacred funeral ceremony?'

Vorgens said, 'I have come to express my sorrow at Okatar's death.'

'Sorrow?'

'His death was not by my order. I did not know of it until after the assassination took place. I did not wish to have him killed.'

'Yet you are the leader of his enemies.'

'Yes,' Vorgens admitted, 'but this battle has gone beyond my control – beyond anyone's control. The war on Shinar has lost its meaning. We are fighting each other now simply for the sake of fighting.'

The Komani said nothing.

'I don't have much in the way of personal possessions to add to the pyre,' Vorgens went on, 'but I do want to give these, as a token of my regret.' He unpinned the diamond insignia clips from the collar of his tunic and handed them to the nobleman.

For a moment, Lensor stood frozen, immobile. Then slowly he extended his massive hand and accepted Vorgens' offering.

'I shall place them on the pyre myself,' he said.

'Thank you. May I stay to witness the ceremony? I could remain at this spot, if you wish.'

The nobleman turned to his fellow council members. None of them objected.

'Very well, you may remain. And – after the ceremony, you will accept our hospitality.'

'Agreed,' Vorgens said. 'Perhaps then we can talk of ways to stop this killing.'

'Yes, perhaps the time has come to talk of peace.'

CHAPTER TWENTY-ONE

A BETTER MAN

Sittas sat in Vorgens' tiny compartment aboard the dread-naught while the Star Watchman packed his few belongings in a travel kit.

'This court-martial that you must face,' the old priest asked, 'is it serious?'

'More than serious,' Vorgens said. 'I may be lucky just to remain in the Star Watch.'

'Even though you have stopped the fighting? Even though the Komani have left Shinar?'

'That will have very little to do with it, I'm afraid. The charges filed by Brigadier Aikens concern insubordination, armed mutiny, personal malice, and a few other items.'

'But the Imperial Senate wants you to report to them, to present the case for Shinar's self-government.'

Vorgens looked up from the travel kit, which was resting on his bunk. 'Yes, I've been ordered to appear before the Senate, together with Clanthas and some of the other Shin-arian leaders, but that's got nothing to do with the court-martial.'

'Still, I doubt that you have much to fear,' Sittas said hopefully.

Vorgens shook his head. 'I'd like to stay in the Star Watch . . . but – I'd do it all over again, if I had to!'

'You were right, and the brigadier was wrong,' Sittas said.

'I was lucky.'

'The Komani have gone. Shinar is at peace.'

'More luck than skill,' Vorgens insisted. 'Okatar's death took most of the fight out of them. The way your own people were fighting helped to make them realize they had no glory to gain here. I guess that handful of reinforcements was the last straw. So the Komani nobles blamed everything on Okatar and went back home.'

'Of course, your hint that more Terran reinforcements

might arrive at any time helped to push them in the right direction.'

Vorgens nodded. 'I wanted to make certain that they knew the Empire was ready and able to defend itself. They took the bait and accepted a path to peace that wouldn't shame them.'

'Therefore, the court-martial must acquit you,' Sittas concluded. 'None of this would have come to pass if Brigadier Aikens had remained in charge.'

'I wish you would be sitting on the bench at the trial,' Vorgens answered, laughing. 'I don't know. Nothing is definitely settled yet. Suppose the Senate decides not to allow Shinar any measure of self-government? Then the court-martial could add treason and sedition to its list of charges.'

He looked around the compartment, satisfied himself that he had everything he wanted, and snapped the kit shut. He opened the door to the passageway.

'Do you seriously believe,' Sittas asked, rising to join him, 'that the Empire will refuse our modest request?'

Vorgens grinned. 'I think they'll listen to Clanthas and agree with him. If they're wise, old friend, you have nothing to fear.'

'Yes,' the priest agreed. 'Sooner or later, wisdom wins through.'

'Sooner or later,' Vorgens agreed. 'But in the meantime a terrible toll of bloodshed can take place. A lot of men – good men – can be sacrificed.'

'The violent ones have had their day on Shinar,' Sittas said. 'Now it is time for a wiser man, a better man, to hold sway.'

'I hope so,' the Watchman said.

They reached the outer hatch and swung it open. The bright, yellow sun sent a shaft of warmth into the passageway. Outside, Vorgens could see the landing ship waiting to take him up to an orbiting starship and then back to Earth. Clanthas and several others were clustered by the base of the ship.

Vorgens clambered down the ladder to the ground, then helped Sittas navigate the metal rungs. He turned around to pick up his travel kit, and found Altai standing beside him.

For the first time since he had met her, she was wearing a dress – simple, feminine, beautiful.

'I – I was wondering if I'd – get to see you,' Vorgens said

Sittas cleared his throat and announced, 'I believe I'll chat with Clanthas for a moment. You two can join me there.'

'Did you think I wouldn't come to see you off?' Altai asked, with a touch of mischief in the corners of her mouth.

'I wasn't certain if you'd get a chance to.'

'I won't say goodbye,' she said, 'because I expect you to return to Shinar before the year is out.'

'That might not be possible,' Vorgens said quietly. 'At any rate, you'll soon have other things to occupy your mind, without worrying about me. Merdon will be out of the hospital soon. By the end of the year, you might even be married.'

'I don't think so,' she said.

'We hardly know each other.'

'We'll have a lot to talk about.'

He grinned at her. 'Yes, I suppose so. All right, I'll be back, then. One way or another.'

They walked together toward the men at the ship. Within a few minutes Vorgens, Clanthas, and the others had boarded. Altai and Sittas stepped back and watched as the ship reverberated with power, took off majestically, and disappeared into the distant sky.

More Great Science Fiction Authors from Sphere

DAMNATION ALLEY

ROGER ZELAZNY

Winner of both the Hugo and Nebula Awards, Roger
Zelazny has created in Damnation Alley a terrifying story
of an odyssey through man-made hell. Damnation Alley is
three thousand miles of radio-active wasteland, torn by
hurricanes and fire storms, the domain of mutants and
monsters. Hell Tanner, the last Angel to survive from the
Big Raid which destroyed most of America, is the only man
with a chance to cross from California with the plague
serum desperately needed in Boston. Damnation Alley
lay directly in his path.

0 7221 9426 9   65p

Now a major Twentieth Century Fox release, starring
Jan-Michael Vincent, George Peppard and
Dominique Sanda.

More Great Science Fiction Authors from Sphere

THE DORSAI TRILOGY

GORDON R. DICKSON

The Hugo Award epic vision of the future, a concept that ranks alongside Asimov's Foundation trilogy in its galaxy-spanning scope.

TACTICS OF MISTAKE

The men of Dorsai were mercenary troops without equal in the universe. But not even they could anticipate the dramatic effect of Cletus Grahame's brilliant mind and the galaxy-shaking theory he called 'The Tactics of Mistake'. To prove his theory he would risk the future of three worlds and the Dorsai themselves.

0 7221 2954 8   60p

SOLDIER, ASK NOT

On New Earth, the black-clad mercenaries of the Friendly planets pitted their religious fanaticism against the cold courage of the Dorsai. Playing one against the other was Tam Olyn, who, in his search to avenge his dead brother-in-law, was ready to use his frightening knowledge of the Final Encyclopaedia.

0 7221 2952 1   60p

DORSAI!

Donal Graeme, Dorsai of the Dorsai, was the ultimate soldier, a master of space war and strategy. With Donal at their head, the Dorsai embarked upon the final, seemingly impossible venture: unification of the splintered worlds of Mankind.

0 7221 2951 3   50p

More Great Science Fiction Authors from Sphere

WAR OF THE WING-MEN

POUL ANDERSON

A sci-fi adventure classic from Hugo Award-winning author Poul Anderson. When three Terrans crash-landed on Diomedes it was clear that their supplies would not carry them across the thousands of miles of unmapped territory to the one Terran outpost. Their only hope was help from the Wing-Men, the barbarian inhabitants of Diomedes.

0 7221 1161 4   60p

THE FALL OF THE TOWERS

SAMUEL R. DELANEY

A saga of stunning imaginative power from the winner of three Nebula Awards. The Empire of Toromon was the last hope of mankind after the Great Fire. Sealed off from the radioactive wastelands, the Empire survived to face new and deadly adversaries – the Lord of the Flames, the berserk Imperial military computer, and an invading alien intelligence in search of conquest.

0 7221 2909 2   95p

All Sphere Books are available at your bookshop or
newsagent, or can be ordered from the following address:
Sphere Books, Cash Sales Department,
P.O. Box 11, Falmouth, Cornwall.

Please send cheque or postal order (no currency), and allow
19p for postage and packing for the first book plus 9p
per copy for each additional book ordered up to a
maximum charge of 73p in U.K.

Customers in Eire and B.F.P.O. please allow 19p for
postage and packing for the first book plus 9p per copy
for the next 6 books, thereafter 3p per book.

Overseas customers please allow 20p for postage and
packing for the first book and 10p per copy for each
additional book.